SHARON A. MITCHELL

MINE

BOOKS

By Sharon A. Mitchell

When Bad Things Happen

GONE

TRUST

SELFISH

INSTINCT

REASONS WHY

MINE

SANCTUM

Vinci Books

vinci-books.com

Published by Vinci Books Ltd in 2025

1

The EU GPSR authorised representative is Logos Europe, 9 rue Nicolas Poussion, 17000 La Rochelle, France
contact@logoseurope.eu

Chapter One

Daniel

It was wrong, all so wrong.

First, they were late. Mom didn't get him up on time. She said she got up early to work on a project, then got so into it she forgot the time. He got that—it happened to him all the time when he was really into something. But gee, Mom. Grown-ups were supposed to have it together. Not getting out of bed at the correct time meant his routine was all messed up, and he had to skip his calming twenty minutes of Lego building time. That was wrong, just wrong.

Then, his red shirt was nowhere to be found. It was Tuesday, so he wore that red shirt. Always. Mom got all in a flap trying to find it. She promised she'd done the laundry and put it away. They finally found the shirt all balled up, trapped between the washing machine and the dryer, still with the grape jelly stain down the front. He didn't care, but Mom said that no, he could not wear it in that condition. So now he had on Thursday's shirt, which would mess things up for later this week.

It was Elizabeth's turn to drive him and his friends to school, but she called to say she was sick. Stuff like that happened, he knew, but still, it threw out their routine. Mom drove them instead. She was an okay driver usually, but this morning she was upset about not waking him up on time, and about the red shirt, so her driving was fast and erratic, not soothing at all. Timothy noticed it and flicked his fingers hard all the way to school, in time with his rocking. Amy didn't seem to care; she chattered the whole way.

Things would be better once he got to the classroom. He liked Ms. Harding; she was a routine kind of person. September had been tough. A lot changed when you moved from grade one to grade two. Not as much of a change as from kindergarten to first grade. Boy, last year was a challenge. But grade two was better. Ms. Harding had routines for *everything*. Once you figured out the patterns, it was comforting to know how things would go.

Daniel froze in the hallway. Behind him, some kid bumped into his back. A shiver went through him, and his fists clenched. Yuck. He hated to be touched unexpectedly.

Something wasn't right. Where was Ms. Harding? She always stood in the doorway to their classroom, giving each student a hug, handshake or high five–their choice. Some kids mixed it up, making a different choice each morning, but not Daniel. He'd made the big decision once and stuck with it. Handshakes were things that people did; he'd studied adults a lot. So that was his choice, something he'd need to get used to all his life.

Hanging back, Daniel watched some of his classmates. At least, he thought they must be his classmates because they entered his classroom. It was sometimes hard to tell because faces often blurred together in a jumble. Unless he spent a lot of time with someone, like his friends, he could get lost in the sea of details and find it hard to recognize individual facial features and match them to a name. He noticed how the kids hesitated in the doorway, looking for Ms. Harding. Then they'd just go into the room and sit down, ignoring that whole hug/hand-shake/high five routine. It wasn't right and had never happened before.

What a day.

Heels clicked, clicked down the hallway. Mrs. Frey, the principal, approached from the other direction. Noticing Daniel lurking behind the door, she motioned to him to follow her in. "Come on, Daniel. Get in the classroom." She used that impatient tone that Mom got when they were late. Maybe Ms. Frey's mother hadn't woken her up on time, either.

Peeking in the classroom doorway, Daniel blinked. The sunshine through the windows seemed brighter than usual. Maybe someone had washed the panes of glass, removing the dust and grime. Too bad. He preferred it when the light was muted.

The fluorescent lights overhead hummed. Some days, that constant buzz was more annoying than at other times. Today was one of the bad times. Maybe that was why the kids were talking so loudly, to be heard over that incessant buzzing.

Click, click, click, click. Ms. Frey hustled around the room. She stopped to say something to a few of the kids, giving that fake smile adults used when they tried to be polite but had their minds elsewhere and didn't really see you. Geez, her high heels were annoying. Why couldn't she wear soft-soled shoes like Mom and Ms. Harding? Click,

click, click. Maybe if she'd just stand still, it wouldn't be so aggravating.

"Daniel!"

From Mrs. Frey's tone, Daniel guessed that she'd called his name several times already. How was he supposed to hear over all the racket in here?

"Daniel, didn't you hear me? I told you to go put your backpack in your cubby."

Yes. No. No, he hadn't heard her before, but yes, he had now. But no. He didn't want to. The weight felt good on his back, calming him amid the chaos that had replaced his usual classroom.

"Daniel!"

He knew that tone. When Mom used it, it meant he had better get moving.

Dragging the palm of one hand flat against the wall, he shuffled his feet toward the cubicles at the back of the room. Keeping the soles of his feet on the floor helped him feel more grounded, as did his hand following the line of the wall, then the blackboard.

Oops. His fingertips snagged a paper and pulled it off its thumbtack. He stooped to pick it up. The name printed on the top said Randy. Randy wasn't one of his favorite kids. Others seemed to like Randy, but he was too loud for Daniel, too in your face. And, he was fast, rarely staying in one place for long and you never knew what he was going to do next. Probably he wouldn't notice this tear in his picture. Carefully, Daniel replaced it on the bulletin board.

"Daniel. What's taking you so long? We're ready to begin and waiting for you to join us."

Shrugging the straps from his shoulders, Daniel stood with his pack in his hands. His back felt naked without the weight. Slowly, he settled the load on the floor of his cubby.

He kept his head and shoulders inside the space for a minute, relishing the wooden barrier that defined his spot. Plus, his name was neatly printed along the cubicle's top shelf. Daniel. His private spot.

There was that click clicking again, but a bit different this time. Mrs. Frey was no longer strutting around the room, but staying in place, tapping her foot on the floor in front of her. Her hands were on her hips and her eyes looked directly at Daniel. They didn't move off him and her mouth was a straight line. Body language, his mom said. Think about what a person's body language might tell you.

It was so weird that people thought that a *body* could speak, telling you stuff. That's what mouths were for, or at least on most people. He, himself, did not talk much, but had ways to get his meaning across that worked for him. It's not that he *didn't* want to speak, it's just that it was so hard. There were all these words jumbled around in his head, but getting them from his brain onto his tongue was another matter. Sometimes it worked, but mostly it didn't. So why bother trying? He got along okay anyway.

Besides, most people talked too much, so maybe if he didn't, it would all even out.

He tuned into the classroom. Mrs. Frey was standing there with her mouth opening and closing. Sometimes when people spoke, it was like waa, waa, waa in his brain with all the soundings running together, making it hard to distinguish the individual parts. It was especially hard at times like now when there was all this background noise - kids whispering, shifting in their squeaky seats, scratching pencils on paper, the buzzing of the ceiling lights, and...

Startled, he felt something slip across his lap. Almost instantly, everything felt better with the weighted pillow across his thighs. Ms. Lori, the EA, smiled and moved behind him. Placing both hands on his shoulders, she pressed down gently, but firmly. Ms. Lori was the educational assistant in the classroom. She understood. Under the pressure of her hands, his shoulders relaxed.

Within a few minutes, he could make sense of Mrs. Frey's words. His anxiety spiked.

What? Ms. Harding wouldn't be here today? How could that be?

Sick, suddenly sick? That wasn't supposed to happen to teachers.

They had a plan in place, Ms. Harding and his mom. If she was going to be away, she told Mom ahead of time. Then he and Mom went over the social story about what would happen when a substitute teacher came into the room. It was never good, but being prepared made it a bit more tolerable.

But this, this was breaking the rules. There'd been no warning. What was he supposed to do?

There was a light rapping on the door to their classroom.

"Ah, here she is now." Mrs. Frey waved a strange lady into their room. "Class, I'd like you to meet Mrs. Stewart. She'll be your teacher for the day." With one of those smiles that aren't really smiles, Mrs. Frey hurried out the door.

No! No, no, no. This was not right. Ms. Harding was supposed to be here. *She* was their teacher. Daniel rocked back and forth in his seat. His shoulder blades whacked against his seat back. The heels of his sneakers banged the underside of his seat, then burst forward, only to swing back again. The force of his movements increased as he clung to the sides of his chair.

"We'll start with roll call. Raise your hand when I call your name."

No! That was not how it was done. It was Nina's turn to call out the names. It said so right there on the board. This was all going so wrong.

"I guess you must be Daniel, the only one who didn't raise his hand."

He had not heard her say his name. He's not heard her call any of their names after that first one, which was done in so not the right way. Poor Nina. She'd missed her turn. It wasn't fair. The tightening in his chest grew bigger, so big it might suffocate him any minute now.

Crouching, Lori said, "It's okay, Daniel. It'll be all right. Come with me and we'll go get a drink." She moved her hand from his shoulder to his hand. He missed the weight on his shoulder and tilted his head to the side, trying to find that comforting pressure again. That was his focus, not the tug on his hand. His breath came in gasps.

"Ms. Lori, please sit down. You're interrupting our class." The reprimand came from the imposter teacher, pretending to be Ms. Harding. "And you, young man," her steely eyes turned to Daniel. "Stop making that noise and stay still in your seat."

Her gaze was awful, just awful and mean. After one quick peek, Daniel could not bear to meet her eyes.

"And look at me when I'm talking to you." How could she not see that she made this impossible? While it had been just tiny squeaks coming from his mouth before, now they were louder, the sounds strung together in one long chain, building and building.

Ignoring the imposter, Ms. Lori pulled on his fist, tucking her other hand under his upper arm, all but lifting Daniel from his seat.

But it was too late, and all too much.

Chapter Two

It was recess time. Gathered in the principal's inner sanctum were the principal, Mrs. Frey, substitute teacher Mrs. Stewart, EA Lori Nabuker, and consultant Mel Nichols. It was tight with all four adults huddled around the speakerphone.

"Hello, Ms. Foster. We've had a little problem this morning."

"What? Is Daniel all right? Have you lost him again? I'll be right there."

Mel interrupted. "Hold on, Keira. It's all right. This is Mel Nichols, the consultant. Daniel is right here, and he's fine."

"What's the problem then?"

Mel continued. "The problem was change and there were a lot of changes this morning, enough to throw Daniel off his game."

Keira knew what that likely meant. "What's he doing now?"

"Hey, Keira. It's Lori."

Some of the tension in Keira's shoulders eased. Lori knew Daniel and could read him well. She was a wonderful EA to have in her son's classroom. "What's going on, Lori?" And, if there was a problem, why wasn't Lori with him?

"Ms. Harding's away today." Lori left it at that, knowing Keira would get the significance.

"But I thought we had a plan in place for her absences. I'd work through the social story with Daniel the night before, preparing him for a substitute teacher. I checked my phone and email last night and there was no message from the school." They all knew how surprise changes threw Daniel. It was in everyone's best interests if they prepared him ahead of time for change.

Principal Frey took over. "We had no time to notify you. On her way to school this morning, Ms. Harding was in an accident was taken to hospital to be checked over."

"Is she all right?"

"Bruised and shaken, so she'll be off for a few days, but she'll be fine, she says."

In the silence that followed, Keira's imagination tumbled over itself, envisioning how Daniel might take the shock of his teacher not welcoming him at the door of their classroom. She was almost afraid to ask. "How did things go?"

"Not well." Before anyone else could speak, a stranger's voice spoke. "This is Gloria Stewart. The principal called me in to take Ms. Harding's place today." She cleared her throat. "I've taught for over thirty years, so have experience with students of all ages. Never have I…"

Mel interrupted. "Keira, this is Mel again. As you can imagine, the shock of not seeing his teacher was tough on Daniel. Because all this happened so quickly, there was not time to brief Mrs. Stewart on the plans for the class in general or for Daniel in particular." The things Mel didn't say echoed loudly in the room.

Keira got it. "Was it bad?"

"This is Lori, and yeah, it wasn't good."

"Where is he now? How is he?"

"He's in the sensory room. One of the other EAs is with him, and he's calmer now."

"I'll be right there to get him." Keira began saving the work on her computer.

"No," said Gloria Stewart. "We were just discussing this. I was the teacher in the room at the time of his tantrum. I don't think we should reward this child with a holiday off from school. I agree he needed to calm down, but now that he's quiet, he should return to class, apologize for creating such a ruckus, and do his work like every other child."

"Thank you for your thoughts, Mrs. Stewart," said Principal Frey. "But you've just met this child. Mel, as the autism consultant, what do you suggest?"

"Keira, you know your son, and of course, it's your call." Mel avoided looking at the substitute teacher. "We know him, too, and if you want my opinion, this morning was too much for him. He's more settled now, but he's drained. If you prefer he stay at school, we'll keep things calm for him, but he might be more comfortable at home for the rest of the day. Now that we know Ms. Harding will be away tomorrow as well, we'll have plans in place. We're already working on them, and I'll be teaching in that classroom tomorrow."

"I'll be there in 20 minutes to get my son."

Chapter Three

At home, Daniel played on the thick Berber carpet, creating action figures with his building blocks. At first glance, he appeared like any other seven-year-old, and most people might think he'd recovered from his morning upset. They might even think that the cranky, old substitute teacher was right, and that Daniel had thrown a fit to get out of doing his schoolwork. As the sub, Gloria Stewart, said during the conference call, what kid wouldn't like to get to go home and play?

Daniel wouldn't, that's who. Keira knew her son. He would not fake a meltdown. He would not purposely do anything to upset his routine, and he knew the regimen to be followed at school.

The tenseness in his neck belied his seemingly unconcerned play. The twitching fingers of his left hand, the way his body started at every squeak of Keira's chair, the way he constantly checked on his mom from the corner of his eye, were all clues that no, Daniel was not all right. He was better than he'd been a few hours ago, but his body was still on high alert.

Thinking of the adrenalin and cortisol that must have run rampant through his small body this morning when he panicked, Keira vowed to do anything to make her child feel safe.

To do that, she needed to stick to their routine, and replicate the environment where Daniel was in his most calm state. That meant getting back to the basics, with just the two of them, in their comfortable, predictable routine. That might mean giving some things up.

Anything. Daniel and his needs came first. She would do anything to protect her son.

That anything included Jake, no matter how much Jake fumed. Oh, he kept his temper in check, but behind his terse words, Keira heard the hurt.

What he asked was nothing unusual. He'd simply called to say he'd be over later and would bring supper, as he did several times a week. Normally, the food and his presence were welcomed by both Keira and Daniel.

Since Jake entered their lives several years ago, they were often now a threesome, rather than the twosome of just Keira and Daniel.

But not tonight.

"I'm sorry, Jake, but it's not a good time."

Silence. "What do you mean?" He spent time with Keira and Daniel more days than not. He'd been there when one of them was sick. On various occasions, he'd held both of them while they puked, washed their faces with a warm cloth, prepared chicken soup. He'd spent hours with Daniel while Keira worked feverishly to meet a contract's deadline. He'd seen them both at their best and at their worst. What did she mean it wasn't a good time? "What's going on, Keira?"

"Daniel had a rough time at school this morning. He needs to be quiet at home for the rest of the day."

Jake looked at the phone. Quiet? Did she think he was a one-man band? He'd spent countless evenings on the couch with Keira and Daniel, watching the endless loops of the videos Daniel so enjoyed. Jake didn't care. Just being there with them, his two favorite people, was enough. "Is he okay?"

"He is now."

"Then what's the problem with me coming over? I planned on bringing his favorite takeout food." Keira could be prickly, but he thought they'd moved past that long ago. "Daniel doesn't mind me. You know that."

It was true. Many times, as the evening wore on, it was Jake's lap Daniel sought, rather than his mom's.

Keira knew Jake and the way his mind worked. Short of hanging up on him, she was going to have to explain. That didn't mean Jake was going to like what he heard. Still, Daniel first... "He had a meltdown at school. I brought him home. When he's been upset like that, we need to go back to the basics, back to the routine he was used to, the one that comforted him."

"Yeah, I get that. I've been around him long enough to know."

True. He got it, at least most times. She did not want to hurt this man, but knew that her next words would do just that. "It needs to be just Daniel and me this evening. He needs to be calm, and know what to expect..."

"What to expect? He expects me to be there. I'm there most evenings, unless I'm working." Jake ran his hands through his hair. "Geez, Keira, I put the kid to bed half the time. He wants me, *me*, to read him his bedtime story." This made no sense. Daniel was used to him, liked him, maybe even loved him, the same way Jake loved this little boy. "Keira, talk to me. Tell me what's going on."

"I'm parenting, Jake. I know what's best for Daniel and best for tonight is just him and me." Her tone changed. "Please understand. I'm just doing what's right for Daniel."

"Yeah? And is this what's right for you, too? For me?"

"Those things don't matter. Only Daniel does and I need to do what I have to do for him."

"How long is my banishment going to last?"

"Jake, don't be like that. Please try to understand."

"How long, Keira?"

"Maybe just for tonight. I need to see how he is tomorrow."

"Fine. Call me tomorrow."

Gently, Keira set her phone back on her desktop. Well, that went about as well as she'd thought it would. A flicker of doubt entered her mind. Was she wrong? Too hard on Jake? After all, Daniel obviously loved the man. The two were close.

Still, this meltdown was a setback. He'd not had one in school at all this year. She needed to get their lives back on an even keel. Consistency and routine were crucial to autistic kids. She'd do what had always worked for them.

Her phone chirped. Jake. He wasn't giving up. At other times, she loved that trait in him, but not this time. She was in mama bear mode and would do what she needed to do for her son.

She glanced at the phone and frowned. Not Jake, but an unknown number. She silenced it.

A self-contained kid, Daniel had always been good at amusing himself. Keira admired that. While other mothers complained they couldn't get a minute to themselves, Keira had the opposite problem. Much of Daniel's toddlerhood had been spent with Keira working to engage him, to have him interact with her.

After his autism diagnosis, things became clearer. She understood why their day did not go well when she put certain clothes on him - clothes with tags or seams that rubbed. They did their shopping first thing in the morning when stores were uncrowded so that he wouldn't get so overwhelmed by the noise and lights and crowds. They frequented the stores that had "quiet shopping hours" where the music was off and the lights less bright.

She learned to go with Daniel's interests and nurture them. Communication was still a challenge, but they'd carved out a good life together, just the two of them.

They'd had to. Everyone else rejected them.

Her phone vibrated. Again. A quick glance ascertained it was not Jake, but an unknown number again. Probably some telemarketer. From across the room, Daniel watched her. Probably wondering why she didn't answer the phone. She silenced it. "Mommy has work to do," she told Daniel.

Did she ever. Grateful that Daniel happily occupied himself, she turned back to her computer monitor. The graphic design contract work she did was ideal for a single mother. She could work around the times when her son needed her. It had been tough in those early years, but she'd gotten the hang of juggling current jobs with the need to pick up new contracts. Working from home suited her and Daniel. Now that he was in school full days, she had more time and her business had picked up, with steady clients recommending her services to new firms. These days, she could even afford to be choosy about which projects she took on.

Her phone vibrated yet another time. Same unknown number. This was getting annoying. Maybe she should turn the phone off, but that went against the grain. For so many years, she'd needed to be available to both clients and the school in case they called her about Daniel. No, she couldn't do it. She silenced the call and shoved the phone to the far corner of her desk.

Like Daniel, Keira could fully focus. It's what let her get so much accomplished, even when she worked in spurts.

Only in a dim part of her consciousness did it register that her pesky phone vibrated with an incoming call. Then it stopped.

Movement out of the corner of her eye snagged her attention. Daniel picked up her phone and held it to his ear.

A male voice came through. "Hello. Hello?"

No, that wasn't Jake's deep timbre.

"Hello, is anyone there? Keira?"

Daniel held the phone out to his mom. Oral communication was not his forte, although he used some words now. This was not one of those times.

Taking the phone from Daniel with a smile of thanks, Keira put the pesky device to her ear. "Hello."

"Keira, is that you? I've been trying to reach you for weeks."

That voice. Something pinged in her memory but didn't make any usable connection. Was it one of her clients? "Who is this, please?"

"It's Mason."

Silence. She only knew one Mason, but that was from long ago. It couldn't be him.

The voice on the phone cleared its throat. "Mason Cooper."

The room around Keira grew smaller. It narrowed to

one focal point - Daniel. The child stood staring at her. She pulled him to her side, placing a kiss on the top of his wavy, reddish hair. There were no words for what the name Mason Cooper did to her.

"Yeah, I know. This is a surprise, right?" He waited. "Keira, can you say something?"

"What do you want?"

He laughed.

Once, long ago, Keira had known this man, that laugh, well. This wasn't his humor laugh, it was his nervous one. "Why are you calling me? And how did you get this number?"

"Gotta admit, you weren't easy to find. But a little effort, a little money, and here we are."

"What do you want from me?" Old feelings erupted in her stomach, pushing their way up, getting caught in her throat. Once, he'd taken everything from her, or that's how it had felt at the time.

"My son, of course."

Chapter Four

That voice. How long since she had last heard it? Wait, she knew exactly how long - Daniel's age, plus six months. Their son's age. No, *her* son's age.

With that voice, the memories tumbled back, over and over each other, the good drowned out by the bad. Those were her darkest days.

College. It had been fun. Moving away from home, taking classes that fit her interests and talents, meeting Mason.

It had been her junior year. The novelty of living in a dormitory had long worn off. Keira was a private person, and the constant presence of others around her was wearying.

When she and Mason started going out together, she spent more and more time at his attic, one-room apartment that was his and his alone. By Christmas of that year, he invited her to move in with him. It only made sense since she was there most of the time, anyway.

Life was good. They got along well and shared the tiny

space with little conflict. Although they didn't talk about permanent commitments, Keira felt like their partnership together was unshakable.

That spring, Mason, who was a year ahead of her, graduated. With his new job came money. Now that he wasn't a poor student, the cramped space irritated him, and he was no longer content to scrimp. Together, they found a better place, bigger, with a kitchen, living room, bedroom, bathroom, and small extra room they called their office. The spaces felt huge compared to the one-room jumble they'd been used to.

It was farther from campus, so Keira had to take two busses, plus walk a bit, but it was worth it to live in such a nice place. Still, with a year of college left to go, Keira's budget was tight. Not a problem, Mason had said. Whereas they used to share in the rent equally, now Mason could pay two-thirds of the cost. That meant that Keira's third taxed her finances, but she picked up more hours at the library where she worked part time. She could handle it for the final eight months of school, then she, too, would have a decent job with more money coming in.

Senior year of college was busy with classes, assignments, as well as working full days on Sunday, and three other 4-hour shifts during the week.

Christmas exams rolled around. Keira's mind was stressed; her body was stressed. But she'd manage, of course she would. Just another five months, then she'd have her degree.

One thing had always been true for Keira - her body followed her mind. When her brain operated in over-drive, her body went out of sync as well. Her menstrual cycle, never perfectly predictable, became irregular when her system became taxed.

When she missed her period in January, the omission didn't register. Final semester. She was busy. She was tired.

When the same thing happened in February, she took note, but thought little of it. This had happened before, lots of times. Plus, she had too much to do, too much she needed to get done to think about anything extraneous.

The flu lingered. It wasn't a violent sort of flu, but one where she felt sick on and off. Food had little appeal, as it didn't stay down well. On the plus side, their toilet bowl was spotless. Since she spent so much time with her head near its rim, she cleaned it at least once a day.

But she was so tired. Just two more months, then school would be over.

Mason, at first supportive of her tummy upsets, grew less patient. "At least go to the doctor, Keira. Get something for it. Barfing several times a week isn't normal, and it stinks up the bathroom."

He was right. It wasn't normal. It signaled an unusual state, one Keira never contemplated happening to her. She was pregnant.

Leaving the doctor's office, she called in sick to work, for the first time ever. She wasn't lying, she truly was nauseous, but now she knew the reason this state plagued her for the last two months. Pregnant. She was going to have a baby, she, and Mason.

Entering the park across the way, Keira found a spot to sit, a place removed from everyone else, a place to contemplate, then savour the news. A baby.

Her initial fear and shock gave way to calm, then a smile. She rested her palm on her still-flat abdomen. A baby. A new life created by the two of them, a new life to cherish and raise together. She smiled to herself, her step lighter as she boarded the bus for home, the nest she and Mason shared.

The smell of bacon frying turned her stomach as Keira opened the door. The popping and sizzling followed behind the aroma of almost burnt toast.

Lovely that Mason was home and had started supper. But bacon? Normally a fan, these last two months changed things. She'd told Mason this, how bacon churned her stomach these days and asked if they could please avoid it. He said it was all in her head. She'd researched to find out why this former fave now sent her gut into revolt. And why bacon? Other meats didn't do it?

But bacon was unique. She'd looked it up at the library. When the fatty acids broke down as it cooked, they turned into compounds of smells and tastes called furans, aldehydes, and ketones. Furans were nutty and sweet, aldehydes grassy, and ketones buttery. Somehow, the combo sent her stomach into rebellion.

She ran to the bathroom to heave.

"You okay, babe?" Mason carefully flipped the bacon strips over so they would cook evenly. A grease bubble popped, and he pulled back his hand, bringing the side of his fist to his mouth, licking the tiny burn spot. "How long is this flu going to last? You need to see a doctor."

Pale, and on the shaky side, Keira emerged from the bathroom and headed to the kitchen sink for a glass of water. "I saw a doctor, and he told me what the problem was."

Mason waited.

"Maybe not exactly a problem, but a reason." Turning to Mason, Keira slid her arms around his waist, a smile of contentment on her face. "Guess what?"

Mason returned her smile and her embrace. "What? Good news, I presume."

She nodded. "Not sure it can get any better than this." Stepping back a half pace so she could see his face, see the joy she knew would be there, she said. "There's a reason my stomach's been so queasy, and I've been tired." Her grin could not get any bigger. "We're pregnant!"

Mason stiffened, his hands frozen in place on Keira's waist. Then his arms fell as he took a pace back. Then two paces, then three. "Say that again."

Her smile slipped a notch. "We're pregnant. The baby will be here in August."

Mason's head shook back and forth. "No." He held up his hands as a barrier between them. "No. This was not part of the plan. No way."

"I know we hadn't planned it, hadn't talked about it, but it happened anyway." Far less sure of herself now, "Aren't you pleased?"

Mason continued to shake his head from side to side as his feet put more distance between himself and Keira. Now he began to pace, striding the length of the living room and back again. Hands fisted on either side of his head. As if talking more to himself than to his girlfriend, he muttered as he paced. "No. No way. I'm not having a kid. I *can't* have a kid. A kid would ruin everything." His strides grew faster and longer.

He stopped directly in front of Keira, his nose just inches from hers. "You're getting rid of it, right?"

Keira's eyes widened, and she stepped back. Who was this man? "No, of course not. I'm past 12 weeks, so it's too late, anyway, even if I wanted to, which I don't." Life was sacred. Hadn't she learned that lesson all her life?

"I'm outa here, then. I want no part of this." Snatching up his jacket, Mason left, the door slamming after him.

Chapter Five

"Your son? *Your* son?" Keira stared at the phone in her hand, then at the seven-year-old playing on the carpet. How dare Mason, the man who had deserted and rejected them, call Daniel his son?

Glancing at the child, she consciously lowered her voice. Daniel was sensitive to moods, and she didn't want him any more upset than he had been earlier that day. Giving her son a smile and a one-armed hug, she left the room. Think. Where best to go? With Daniel's acute hearing, she didn't want him listening to even this one-sided conversation.

Upstairs in the bathroom, she turned on the faucet and sat on the side of the tub. The noise of the running water should mask her words in case Daniel came by to listen. "Okay. What is this all about, Mason, and make it quick. I'm busy."

"What, no how are you, long time no see and how's your life been and all that?"

Controlling her breathing, Keira unclenched her jaw before replying. "I don't care how your life's been. After the way you ran out on us, I never want to hear of you or your existence again. Goodbye and good riddance."

Too bad she didn't have one of those old, corded phones from the 80s, one that she could actually slam back onto a receiver. Somehow, pushing the red disconnect button on a smart phone didn't have the same panache.

Keira realized she was trembling. And cold, oh so cold. She tried to beat back the images from the darkest time of her life, but they persisted, breaking through the barricades she'd fought so hard to erect.

She turned off the faucet, but the running water gave her an idea. Leaving the bathroom, she checked on Daniel, telling him she was going to take a bath. She pressed play on his favorite video. Yeah, she knew that television was a terrible babysitter, but when needs must… He'd be content for at least 45 minutes, maybe more if he watched it over again.

After ensuring that the front and back door were locked, she returned her phone to the charger on her desk and gathered her comfiest flannel pajamas. She hesitated. Oil or bubble bath? She added a generous dollop of lilac-scented oil, then two, but bubbles would be good, too. Scanning the bottles lined up on the side of the tub, she chose lavender bubble bath. Lilac and lavender - both L words, both flowers, both *purple* flowers. How could they not work well together? She dumped in several dollops, waited a few moments, then added more. Why not? She needed all the comfort she could get while she allowed her thoughts to stray to Mason and the worst year of her life.

Disrobing, Keira gathered her hair into a loose knot on top of her head, then sank into the warm, silky, fragrant water.

Only then did she let the tears come.

Rarely did Keira feel sorry for herself. Holding a pity party was not her style. She should know - she'd tried it and it hadn't helped, not one whit.

Visions of the night Mason fled rolled over her.

When he had left, slamming the door, Keira ran after him. He heard her, she knew he did, yet his stride didn't slow. He almost ran to his motorcycle, hopped on, and sped away, without one glance back at the woman who held him in the center of her world.

Back in their suite, Keira shut, but didn't lock the door. Somehow, with it unlocked, it seemed more inviting for Mason's return. And she knew he would return. Of course he would. He was just shocked.

Well, she'd been shocked herself when the doctor told her the results of the pregnancy test. Shocked, because the possibility never occurred to her, and she'd not given much thought to having kids. Maybe one day, in that hazy future, but her life and babies were not strands she'd thought of weaving together.

But as she left the medical clinic with a prescription for prenatal vitamins in her hand, a small smile came to her lips. Then a bigger one.

No, it wasn't planned, but not everything in life was. She'd be finished her degree before the baby was born. Mason had a good job, they had a nice place to live with plenty of room for an infant, and within the next year Keira would start her career as well.

The nurse practitioner talked about baby hormones. She explained that the fatigue Keira experienced was normal, and many pregnant women felt they were more emotional than usual.

That was it. That was the reason Keira sank to the floor by the unlocked door and sobbed.

It was probably her fault. She had not broken the news to Mason very well. She should have warmed up to the announcement. She should have reassured him it was going to be all right, that she could handle this, that *they* could handle it. Surely, he'd come to love the idea as much as she did already.

A draft on her back woke Keira. She stretched, trying to ease into a more comfortable position. The crack under the door let in a cool breeze. How had she never noticed that before?

It was dark in the apartment. When she'd cried herself into an exhausted sleep, it had been light out. Now it was night. Had Mason returned without waking her?

"Mason," she called.

Nothing.

Using the doorknob for leverage, Keira hoisted herself to her feet, reaching for the light switch. She blinked as light flooded the kitchen and entryway. "Mason," she called again. She checked the living room, the bedroom, the study, and the bathroom. No, she was alone. Where was Mason? He rarely stayed out this late, and not without letting her know where he'd be.

Her phone. Of course. She must have slept right through it, ringing or the chime of a text message. Messages. There were likely several of them, since it was almost six hours ago that Mason had left.

Digging through her purse, she pulled out her phone. Nothing. Yes, it was charged, but there was not one text from Mason, and no missed calls.

Poor guy. He must be really upset. How could she have just blurted out the news like that? She prepared a sandwich for him, covered it in plastic wrap, and set it in the fridge. She put a note on the table, letting him know to look for the sandwich. Then she washed her face and headed to bed.

The next morning, she'd woken up alone. A search of the apartment showed no evidence that Mason had returned. Shaken and hungry from skipping supper the day before, Keira gulped down some milk and a banana, then tried to repair the ravages hours of crying had left on her face.

No matter how she felt or looked, she had to go to class. It was the final semester of her final year, not the time to slack off. Brushing her hands over her midsection, Keira realized that now, more than ever, it was crucial to finish her schooling.

It was late afternoon before Keira returned to their apartment. As she unlocked the door, she called, "Mason." Then she listened to the silence. She comforted herself knowing that it would be unusual for Mason to be home from work this early. She busied herself with browning meat and preparing supper. Tonight, they'd have a good meal, then sit down and really talk about this. They'd snuggle on the couch and plan. It would be good.

Six o'clock came. Seven o'clock, then nine. Still no Mason. She'd called his cell phone countless times, but her calls went to voicemail, her texts unanswered. Something must have come up at work.

Finally, she wrapped up their dinner, stowing the uneaten food in the fridge. Stifling a yawn, she went into their bedroom. A shower would help. Or maybe a bath.

Opening a dresser drawer, she reached in for a fresh nightgown, noticing something odd. Mason's drawer was not fully shut. Really odd. Mason had a thing about that. It irked him when drawers or cupboards were not fully closed. A quirk of his, for sure, but one she could live with. But why was *his* drawer slightly open? *She* might make that mistake, but not Mason. As she went to shut it for him, she could see the wooden bottom to the drawer. That drawer was full of his socks and underwear. Why did she not see the usual jumble?

Yanking it open, she saw it was empty. What? She pulled open the other drawers he used. All empty. Rushing to the closet, her eyes took in the barren left side of the closet rod. Gone. What happened to Mason's clothes?

Next, she checked the bathroom. Gone. All of Mason's toiletries were missing.

With dread filling her bones to the marrow, her feet dragged their way into the study that they shared. Pulling open the closet door, she saw that Mason's suitcases were no longer stacked in the corner. Whirling, her eyes scanned the desk. His laptop wasn't there; neither was his printer nor any of the things he cluttered their shared space with. Gone. All of it. Just like Mason.

Chapter Six

Knowing she had a few minutes to herself while Daniel watched a movie, Keira laid a warm washcloth over her eyes and rested her head against the folded towel on the back of the tub. Enough sniveling. That era of her life was over. She'd come out of it, *they'd* come out of it just fine, no thanks to anyone else. She and Daniel had survived and even flourished. They were strong, the two of them. Survivors. A team. They didn't need anyone else, and certainly not that scum Mason Cooper.

She relaxed, letting her mind drift, dragging it back from the dark memories every time they'd enter her consciousness. This was a strategy she'd learned during those scary, lonely months of pregnancy, and Daniel's first year of life when she didn't know how she'd manage to provide for them.

A knock on the door interrupted her thoughts. A glance down reassured her that the only parts of her not buried in bubbles were her head and the top of her shoulders. "Come in."

Daniel entered. In his outstretched hand was her cell phone. The thing emitted sounds of a male voice saying, "Hello. Hello? Keira? Anybody there? Are you ignoring me, Keira?"

Pulling her arm from beneath the bubbles, she wiped her hand on a fluffy towel, one of her few indulgences, then reached for the phone. "Thanks, son. I'll be out soon. Then let's have some mac and cheese, okay?"

Returning her smile, Daniel left the room, shutting the door behind him.

Keira waited to hear his retreating steps on the staircase before raising the cell to her ear. She'd forgotten how gabby Mason was. That had always been a contrast to her quieter ways. Maybe that gregariousness had been part of his appeal. Right now, though, she could not see what she'd ever seen in the man.

His voice was still going on. "Keira, are you ignoring me? I heard you talking to someone. You can't ignore me."

Oh, that was precious. "Exactly why can't I ignore you? Why shouldn't I, the way you ignored us?"

"You can't hold that against me."

Keira looked at the phone in disbelief.

Mason continued. "I was a stupid kid back then. You can't blame me. Anyone would have been scared in my position."

"Yeah, I was scared, too."

Mason paused, but only for a few seconds. "But you're good at stuff like that. You handle things. Me, I was just starting my career. I was not prepared to look after someone else. Cripes, Keira, it was all I could do to look after me." He lowered his voice. "You know that. You pretty much organized our life, and I just went along with it."

Is that how he saw things? She'd just done what had to

be done. Somebody had to clean the place. Someone had to do the grocery shopping so there'd be food in the house. Someone had to pay the bills on time.

Mason carried on. "Besides, you had your family. I had no one but my grandmother, and she'd have killed me if she knew I had a kid without being married."

Keira let that hang in the air. Did he even listen to himself?

"I admit I reacted. I could have handled things better back then, but you can't hold it against me."

"Oh, but I can, and I do."

"I've changed. I've grown up. That was almost eight years ago! Things are different now."

"Yes, they are. I'm no longer a frightened student, alone, with a child to bring up by myself."

"Yeah, about that. What's with the kid? I presume he's who answered the phone, but he wouldn't speak to me, not even a hello."

"I guess it means he has good taste."

"Keira, don't be like that."

What planet was he from? "Why are you bothering me now, Mason?"

"I told you. I want my son."

"You have no son. You lost the right to call him that when you walked out on us."

"I've explained that. Sheesh. Are you going to hold that against me forever? He's my son, and I have rights."

Ludicrous. "I had rights, too. I had the right to be supported while I carried your child. I had the right to child support all these years. What happened to those rights, Mason?"

"I can make that up to you. I have money now. What will it take?"

What? He wanted to buy his way into her son's life? Like *that* was ever going to happen.

"Look, why don't we start simply. I'd like to meet Daniel. He should know his dad. Can we at least do that?" He waited. "Keira? You still there? Look, we can do this the easy way or the hard way."

"What do you mean?"

"He's my child and I want him. You can agree to this nicely, or I'll go the legal route if I have to."

Legal? How many times during her pregnancy had the nurse practitioner told her she had legal recourse, that the father could be forced to pay child support, to help with her medical expenses? No, Keira had refused. If Mason did not want to be with them willingly, she wanted no part of him or his money.

"Why? Why now?" Had Mason suddenly grown a heart? A conscience?

"Things are different now. I'm in a relationship. We're ready for kids. We want him."

"Well, you can't have him." Did he think Daniel was some toy they could pass back and forth?

"Look, Keira, I can, and I will."

Pressing the button on the side of the phone, she powered it off, then sunk back beneath the bubbles. But the water was cooling, and the comforting cocoon of soothing water no longer felt like the haven it had been. Damn Mason.

The evening passed quietly. Too quietly. She missed Jake. So did Daniel, even asking for him several times. Words did not come easily to this child and the fact that he said Jake's name aloud spoke volumes.

When had the man become such an integral part of their lives? Oh, it had happened slowly, over a couple of years. But more importantly, *why* had she allowed it to happen? She knew better than to rely on a man, or anyone else, for that matter. Mason's call, *calls* reinforced that. How could she forget? No, life was safer when she depended only on herself. She was enough for herself and her son.

Daniel was bathed and in bed, ready for his nighttime story. But, after choosing his book, rather than snuggling into the covers, he leapt from the bed, running from room to room. He returned minutes later, carrying her cell phone. Handing it to her, he said one word. "Jake."

Four or five evenings a week, Jake spent the twilight hours with them. When he couldn't be there, he phoned. He and Daniel would have their one-sided conversation, with Jake talking and Daniel smiling. Then, with her son tucked into bed, she and Jake would spend the next while chatting about their day and, well, just about everything else under the sun. Usually quiet and used to keeping to herself, Keira had found herself opening up to Jake more and more. Now, it felt like he saw the real her. The only time she'd let herself be this vulnerable before had been with Mason. And he'd run. So far, Jake hadn't.

But Daniel was getting too attached to him. So was she, if she allowed herself to think too much about it. Was this fair to Daniel? She never wanted him to go through the pain she'd felt when Mason had deserted her. Protecting her son was her priority, her responsibility.

Looking into her son's eyes, she read the pleading there. Even without using words, Daniel communicated his point. He wanted to hear Jake's voice. So did she.

Oh, what could it hurt? This had been a rough day for Daniel, rough for her, too. They could ease back a bit from Jake starting soon. But not tonight.

She swiped up with her finger. The cell phone didn't

respond. Oh, right. She'd shut it off in the bathroom, ending Mason's call. She powered the thing back on. Missed calls. There were two more from Mason and three from Jake. He'd wonder why she didn't answer. Quickly, she pressed his name on her phone, then listened to the ringing.

"Keira! What's going on? I was giving you ten more minutes, then I was coming to check on you guys."

"Sorry. I'd turned my phone off, then forgot to turn it back on."

"Are you okay?"

"Yeah. Here's Daniel. He wants to say goodnight." She passed the phone to her son. Knowing she had a few minutes while the males chatted, she went to tidy the bathroom after the bubble fight they'd had during Daniel's bath. She heard Daniel's laugh in response to something Jake must have said to him, the same laugh he'd given twenty minutes ago when he blew bubbles from his hands onto Keira's face.

Returning to the bedroom, she saw Daniel laying on his side, snuggled into his pillow, the weighted blanket pulled up to his neck. Beside him sat the phone. "What, no story?" Daniel always had a bedtime story.

Daniel just gave a sleepy smile.

From the phone came Jake's words. "I already read him *Goodnight Moon*. I've read it to him so many times, it's etched in my brain, so I recited it. It must have worked, because when I finished, he said, 'Night'".

"Yep, it must have worked. I think he's asleep already." She pulled his door almost all the way shut and entered her own bedroom. She headed for the rocking chair, pulling a soft cashmere blanket over herself.

"Would it work for *you*? Want me to read you a bedtime story?"

Oh, if it was only that easy. Comfort would be a long time coming tonight. She changed the subject. "How was your day?"

"Keira, let's not do this. My day was a day, but it didn't end the way I thought it would. Why didn't you want me coming over? What's going on?"

Daniel. It was safer to talk about Daniel. Jake would understand that. "Daniel had a bad day at school, a bad morning. His teacher wasn't there, and no one had prepared Daniel for that. Then he had a substitute teacher who didn't get him, who didn't stick to the routine, who tried to make Daniel comply, and it was all too much. He had a major meltdown."

"Ah, sorry to hear that. Poor guy. I thought they had plans in place for when there'd be a sub."

"They do, but this was unexpected, so things sort of unravelled on their end, then for Daniel, too. I brought him home to get him settled."

"What's that got to do with me and why didn't you want me coming over?"

"It's easier to get him calm when it's just him and me, to get us back into his routine."

Silence. Then, "I thought *I* was part of his routine."

Chapter Seven

The rest of the week passed uneventfully. Although not seriously injured, Ms. Harding was sore and needed to rest. She took two more days off school and in her absence, Mel Nichols took her place. She understood Daniel, plus he was prepared for the disruption of how he expected his school day to look. Perhaps he was quieter than usual both at school and at home, and more on guard, but generally back to his normal self.

Keira's days went the way as did Daniel's. If he was happy, then she was content. Her goal for him was a worry-free childhood, where he knew he was loved and enough, exactly as he was.

While some people disliked the isolation of working from home, for Keira and Daniel, it worked. Carved into a corner of the living room was her office. Maybe not ideal for some, but for her and Daniel, it worked.

With Daniel in school full-time, Keira could take on more contracts than when he was younger and needed more of her time. Finances were much less of a concern now. In fact, their lives in general were more relaxed. The thought flitted through her mind that Jake might play a role in that. Nah, while the man was a bonus, it was she and Daniel who had evolved into a workable duo.

Damn. There was her phone again, vibrating away. She dared not turn the thing off in case the school tried to contact her. A quick glance told her it was that same unknown number that had been calling incessantly - Mason. As if she wanted to talk to him again, not ever in her life. The nerve of the guy thinking he could waltz back into their lives and have anything to do with Daniel. Like *that* was ever going to happen. As soon as she got a minute, she'd block that number from her phone.

The doorbell rang, interrupting Keira's concentration. Daniel would be home from school in about 90 minutes. She needed to get this section completed before then. She ignored the bell.

The ringing came again. And again.

With a sigh, Keira pushed back from her desk and walked to the door. The peephole revealed a man in a uniform. After some of the experiences her friends had been through, they were all careful about security these days. She pressed the button on the speaker system. "Yes?"

"Am I speaking to Keira Foster?"

"Yes."

"I have a delivery for you."

"Place it on the step, please, and I'll get it later."

"Sorry. I have to hand-deliver this."

How annoying. A glance at her watch showed time passing quickly. She didn't have time for this. Keira undid the lock and opened the door. "Fine. Do I need to sign something?"

Brushing his long, slightly greasy hair from his eyes, the

fellow thrust a clipboard toward her, showing with a pen where she should write her name. Taking it back with a thanks, he handed over a legal-sized brown envelope.

Using her back to push shut the door, she remembered to set the lock before looking at the return address. A legal firm she'd never dealt with. Must be a mistake, or maybe, something to do with her parents. Her heart sped up. Nah, they didn't even know where she lived and would never bother to look for her.

Slipping a fingernail under one edge, Keira opened the envelope. Out came an official-looking paper with attachments. On top was a handwritten note paper clipped to the stack.

> Keira,
>
> I told you we could do this the hard way or the easy way. If you'd answered any of my calls or texts, we could have handled this easily, just between ourselves.
>
> Your choice.
>
> Now you've forced me to go the legal route.
>
> Here are the papers from my lawyer. This is the semi-easy way. If you still don't come to your senses and comply, the next step is a court-ordered paternity test.
>
> Mason

Underneath the offensive note was a page of legal jargon telling her Daniel was required to take a DNA test to prove paternity. Enclosed was a testing kit with instructions.

Her butt contacted the side of her desk. Good thing, as it held her up. She scanned the page again, more slowly this time. That snake! That rat. Why was he doing this now? Why did he care when he'd never given her or Daniel a thought all these years?

A paternity test. Did he think she'd slept around while living with him? He didn't know her very well if he even considered that possibility. Besides, what did he care? It's not like she'd come after him demanding child support. Never! If he hadn't wanted them, then they'd make it on their own just fine without him.

Who cared if Mason thought he was Daniel's biological father or not? The papers made a satisfying thunk as she tossed them into the trash can under her desk.

Chapter Eight

Tossing Mason's letter into the trash was one thing. Eliminating knowledge of the letter's contents from her mind was something else.

Over the years, Keira learned to compartmentalize. Her brain only had so much capacity, and in order to get things done, she had to stow some worries away and deal just with the present. Things she could control. That's what she needed to focus on.

So why couldn't she do that with Mason? There were other emotionally laden things that had affected her life, but she'd shoved them away. Those ghosts rarely returned to haunt her.

But Mason? Maybe because he was her first love. Maybe because he instigated the biggest disappointment of her life, and the greatest despair. Maybe because a part of him lived on in her household and always would through Daniel.

No, she needed no paternity test to know that Mason had helped create Daniel. And so would Mason if he got

41

even one look at their son's freckles, red hair, and impish grin.

That would never happen, though, not if she had any say in it. The nerve of the man, wanting to meet Daniel. Hell, no. He was late, almost eight years too late to take an interest. They might have needed Mason then, but most definitely had no use for him now.

Still, why now? Why on earth would Mason contact her now? If his biological clock was ticking, why didn't he just go have kids with someone else, someone who wanted him? Why did he have to want *her* son? Guilty conscience? Yeah, well, he was a little late with that. No way was she going to assuage his conscience. He'd acted like scum; let him wallow and deal with it on his own.

The sounds of small feet thumping onto the porch preceded the ringing of the doorbell. Habit had Keira checking the peephole before unlocking the door. Elizabeth waited there with one arm around Daniel and the other around her own son, Timothy. Just in front of the boys stood Amy, the daughter of Elizabeth's neighbor and their friend Cynthia. Keira, Elizabeth, and Cynthia took turns taking the three kids to school and picking them up. This week was Elizabeth's turn.

"Hey," said Elizabeth, as she followed the kids inside. "I'd ask if you're still up for this play date, but it's a little late to check." All three kids had kicked off their shoes, dropped their backpacks and raced off to Daniel's room.

"Yeah, it's fine. Their snacks are ready, and they play so well together." From upstairs, they could hear Amy's voice. Both Timothy, age 6, and Daniel were autistic and verbal communication was a struggle for them. Not so for Amy at all. Her mom, Cynthia, said Amy was born gabbling and had not stopped once in all her 8 years.

Elizabeth stared at her friend. "All right. What gives?"

Keira hedged. "What do you mean?"

"I know you. What's wrong?"

Both Elizabeth and Keira were solitary souls; circumstances had forced that self-preservation skill. Only in the last few years had they made tentative steps toward trust, toward letting others in. Their circle of friends was now tight, and they'd learned to rely on one another.

Plus, Elizabeth's new husband, Brendan, was Jake's best friend and cop partner. Brendan had complained that Jake was like a bear these last few days. Could the same thing eating Jake be bothering Keira?

At first Keira's eyes narrowed and her shoulders tensed at Elizabeth's probing questions, her instinct to push everyone away. But this was Elizabeth. With an audible breath, she let her shoulders slump. Maybe talking about it would help. "Come on," she said.

Leading the way to her desk, she checked that the kids remained upstairs, then pulled the papers from her trash can, handing them to Elizabeth.

Scanning the handwritten note, Elizabeth's eyes dropped to the signature. "Who's Mason?"

"Daniel's father."

Elizabeth's eyebrows rose unnaturally high. "Father? How come I've never heard of him?"

"Father's not really the right term to describe him. He ran out on us as soon as he learned I was pregnant."

Elizabeth waited, knowing there was more to the story.

"And that's the last I've heard from him until a week ago."

This time, just one of Elizabeth's eyebrows tilted.

"I got these calls and texts from an unknown number. I ignored them. Then Daniel answered my phone and

43

brought it to me. It was Mason, and he wanted to meet Daniel."

"Like he has any right to that." Elizabeth's dry tone comforted.

Ah, Elizabeth got it. Keira knew she would. "He seems to think he has some rights." She indicated the papers. "Then this arrived this afternoon."

Quickly, Elizabeth smoothed out the balled-up pages and skimmed the sheets. "The bastard." She looked up. "Just because he wants to meet Daniel doesn't mean he gets to. Does it?"

Keira shook her head.

"And this paternity test stuff. You don't have to do it, right?"

"I don't think so. How could he force it? He ran. He didn't want any part of us. So why now?"

"Good question. Do you think he can force this legally?"

"I don't know."

"What are you going to do?"

Keira's laugh held no humor. "So far, all I've done is throw the papers in the trash. And worry."

"We need to know your options. What does Jake say?"

"He doesn't know about it."

Silence. Okay. Elizabeth knew to abandon that topic. "What could be this guy's motivation? Guilt? Although if he'd been feeling remorse, why wait eight years to do anything about it?" She thought for a minute. "What kind of guy is he, apart from being a chicken scumbag? What's the downside to him meeting Daniel?"

Keira's mama bear instinct rose instantly. "No way! He's never getting near my son." Fear lay just beneath her anger. "What if he wants access to him? To be part of his life? To share custody? I've heard of stuff like that happening."

Elizabeth and Keira shared a look. They both knew that many people didn't understand autistic kids. Both women were protective of whom they allowed into their sons' lives. They had to be.

"What are you going to do?" Elizabeth asked.

"I could run. I could take Daniel and disappear so Mason can never find us again."

Chapter Nine

After Elizabeth collected Amy and Timothy, Daniel looked at his mother expectedly. Supper time, his eyes said. Yeah, except that Keira had nothing planned. Last night they'd had a quick meal of mac 'n cheese, but how many times could she get away with that? Comfort food, for sure, but they needed some variety in their diet, no matter how much Daniel would have been okay with the same meal day after day.

She really didn't feel like cooking, though.

"Come on," she told Daniel. "Put on your shoes. How does a charcuterie sound?" There was a Char Cut Roastery in the mall that served great takeout charcuterie Daniel loved. Each different food came in its own separate sectioned tray - no two items actually touching each other. A small platter was the perfect size for the two of them, with an assortment of meats, cheeses, crackers, and veggies that allowed them to nibble away until they were full.

Entering the mall, Daniel lagged behind. Keira admonished him to keep up when she noticed him walking oddly, his steps lacking his usual agility. Frowning, she watched. No, he wasn't really limping; he put both feet down awkwardly. "Daniel, is there something wrong with your feet?"

He nodded.

"What?"

"Hurt."

"What part hurts?"

He held up his hands with his fingers stretched out, then curved the fingers inward. Then he exaggerated his steps, pushing down with a fist to match each tread.

It took Keira a minute. Toes. Did he mean his toes curled up in his shoes? Kneeling, she pressed her fingers to the toe of each shoe. Yes, she could feel the outline of the raised toes. "Wiggle your toes," she instructed.

Daniel shook his head.

Keira could feel the pressure of something moving under her fingers, but not the normal feel of a child moving his toes up and down. Crikey. The kid's shoes were too small for him? How had she not noticed? Looks like she was out of the running for mother-or-the-year award. Again.

"Let's go buy you some new shoes."

Daniel resisted the pressure of her hand. He hated new clothing, or any sort.

Keira understood and had a plan. "Remember when we bought these?" She pointed at the offending sneakers. "We bought exactly the same shoe you had before, just a size bigger. We'll try to do the same thing again. All right?"

Daniel nodded, but with obvious reluctance. You never knew how new thing might feel. Or smell.

There was an athletic store in the mall, plus a shoe store. Surely one of them would have what they needed. Keira stuck to one particular brand of sneakers, making sure it was popular, to increase the chances of buying the same thing time after time, just in larger sizes.

Daniel's footsteps slowed as they passed Char Cut Roastery.

"Good idea, son. We'll put in our order first, then it will be ready by the time we buy your shoes."

Now that Daniel could read, he took more interest in perusing the menus in places. He pointed to one word he couldn't sound out.

"Habanero," she read to him. "That's a kind of hot pepper. You've tasted one before, but you made a face when you took a tiny bite. You might like it with cream cheese, though."

Daniel went back to reading the menu. When the server approached the counter, Keira nodded for Daniel to point out the items he wanted included in their charcuterie board, then added a few extra of her own favorites. She gave her name, paid, then explained that they'd be back in about 20 minutes to pick it up.

Daniel reached for his mom's arm to check her watch. He made note of when 20 minutes would be up.

Luck was with them. The athletic store had the brand and style of sneakers Daniel wore, plus in one size and two sizes larger. At her request, the clerk pulled both. Pulling off his shoes was not a problem, but Daniel braced himself at the thought of sliding his feet into a new pair. He glanced at his mom. Yes, she was going to insist on this. He took a big breath as Keira stood behind him, putting downward pressure on his shoulders to help ground him as he prepared himself for this new sensation.

Okay, his foot was in. Now the shoe salesman laced

them up, but not properly. A squeal escaped Daniel's tightly pressed lips.

"He likes them tied quite tight, please."

The salesman obliged, then asked Daniel to stand on the floor. The man pressed his fingers into the toe box, instructing Daniel to wiggle his toes. Daniel complied, but pulled back, resting his back against his mother, avoiding any possible touch with this strange man invading his personal space.

Looking at Keira, the salesclerk said, "There's a bit of room, but not much. If he's in a growth spurt, you might want to go up a size."

Oh, lord love a duck. Was this guy insinuating that her son had been wearing shoes not just one size too small, but two? Guilt filled her innards. What kind of a mother was she?

Glancing away as the man swapped out these shoes for another pair, Keira felt eyes on her. Through the glass window of the store, a solitary woman stood staring in at her. The woman's eyes roved from Keira's face to Daniel's.

Instinctively, Keira gathered her son to her. No. No, it couldn't be. She had not seen this person since before Daniel was born. Since she had been three months pregnant with him, to be exact.

She looked again. It was her. Her face lined now, much more so than almost eight years ago, and her once wavy, auburn hair was now mostly steely in color. Her mother.

Images from her childhood flashed through her mind. Sunday dinners. Twinkling lights and presents under the Christmas tree. The solitary swing dangling from the sycamore tree in the backyard. And stranger still were the smells that flooded her senses. The creamy, sweet, cinnamon aroma of her mom's rice pudding, the Yardley's lavender talcum powder her mother applied liberally after every bath, the… She quickly tamped down those memories.

A part of Keira was hungry for a glimpse of the woman who had given birth to her, who had been a daily part of her life for her first 18 years, who was still important to her until that day Keira had confessed to her parents that she was pregnant.

In the woman's eyes was the same yearning that spoke to Keira's soul. No, her parents had made their choice, her mother siding with her father, or certainly not taking Keira's part. Nope, they had made their feelings clear.

She wrenched her gaze from the window, turning her shoulder so that only her profile could be seen from the hallway of the mall, covering Daniel as best she could with her arms, gathering him to her, protecting him. Never would he experience the hurt and pain Keira went through long ago.

Clutching a bag containing Daniel's former toe-crunching shoes, Keira peeked out the door, checking both directions. This wasn't like her. Nothing intimidated her, or so she liked to believe. It was just more convenient if she didn't run into her mother.

The coast was clear. All they needed to do was pick up their food, then make it to their car. When did running out for takeout get so stressful?

Hurrying their steps, Keira felt a tug on her arm. Daniel planted his new sneakers firmly underneath him and refused to budge. He pulled up his mother's sleeve to check the time on her watch.

Daniel shook his head, his eyes going between her watch and her face. His head moved from side to side again. It was not time. It had only been 16 minutes.

Raising her eyes to the ceiling, Keira let air out the

corners of her mouth. Yeah, she knew she had told the server they'd be back in 20 minutes to pick up the food. But sheesh.

A prickly sensation covered her skin. Almost like a magnet, her eyes were drawn to the food court where a lone woman sat, her gaze drinking in the sight of Keira and Daniel. A tentative smile flit across the woman's face, faded, then returned. She half rose from her chair.

Grabbing Daniel by the arm, Keira whirled him around, marching him in too long strides out the far exit of the mall. They'd circle around the outside and go back in the other entrance to grab the food.

Yes, that would make them late. The air reeked of ozone, that scent that heralded one of San Diego's rare rains. They skirted a puddle pooling on the asphalt.

It would take more than the remaining four minutes to navigate their way through the parking lot and back to the other entrance, but Daniel would just have to suck it up and miss their 20-minute mark. Better messing up his sense of time and accuracy, then messing up his life by letting him see the woman who had rejected his very existence.

Chapter Ten

Lounging on the couch with her son, the drapes closed, a Himalayan salt lamp glowing in the corner, doors and windows locked up tight, Keira could almost believe that they were secure in their safe enclave. On the coffee table between them rested the charcuterie board, half picked over. Daniel continued to munch away, but Keira was done. The lead in her stomach had receded somewhat, but left little room for food.

Daniel's eyed were glued to the Lego movie. How Keira envied her son's ability to get lost in the moment. Whereas she, well, she was drowning in the past.

Eight years ago, the week after Mason's desertion had been the worst of her life. At first, her brain denied the evidence of the empty closets and drawers. Yeah, his stuff was gone, but that was just a reaction. He'd think about it and be back, apologizing, pledging his love and support to the budding family they'd created.

After a week of blocked calls and no Mason, reality had nudged its way in. It was almost the first of the month, and rent would be due in six days. Keira didn't have the money. What she made at her part-time job didn't cover the rent, even if she devoted her entire paychecks to it. Mason, with his full-time, well-paying career, coughed up two-thirds of the rent.

The money went into their joint account automatically and Keira paid the rent bill from that. Although he was the one with an economics minor, he really wasn't all that good with money, so Keira handled their bills. It's not that Mason was exactly careless about finances, it's just that dates and times and amounts were pesky details to him, oft overlooked, another of those things you'd get to when you had time.

He wasn't greedy, though, and had no problem with bearing the brunt of their expenses, at least until Keira graduated next spring. She'd be happier when they were on a more even footing with sharing the expenses of their life together.

As was her habit, Keira checked her personal bank account, plus their shared one every day. The first of the month approached. Surely Mason's money would appear in their account on time, the same as it had since they'd moved in together.

It didn't.

The first rolled around, rent was due, and she was short. Even if she drained her other accounts and pooled all her savings, she still didn't quite have enough for the rent. Plus, if she used every cent she had to make the rent payment, she'd have no money for her cell phone bill, bus fare to get to work, or for food. She pressed her palms to her belly. Even if she didn't feel like it, she had to eat for this little one who depended on her.

The first of the month came and went. So did the

second, the third and the fourth. None of her calls or texts to Mason went through.

Returning home from school on the fifth day, Keira found a crisp, cardboard notice slid half under the door to their apartment. A warning. Rent was five days overdue. As per the lease agreement, after a week, there would be an eviction notice.

Options, options, options. That's all Keira's brain had considered over the past week. Try as she might, she could come up with nothing else. Hating to return home with her tail between her legs, Keira had no other choice.

She went to see her parents.

An only child, Keira had grown up in a strange sort of house - a quiet house. Yes, her parents had loved her, she was sure of that, at least in their own way. They provided for her, taught her manners, and all the necessities of life were there. But demonstrative? No. Not in the way she was with Daniel, enjoying the cuddles, making sure in every way that he knew he was loved and cherished.

Keira had no memories of either of her parents playing with her. Yes, she had toys, but she played with them alone. A pallor or gloom hung over the house, almost a funereal quiet. Instinctively, Keira knew that this was not a home that condoned running or yelling.

They were proud of her; she was sure. At least they'd attended her high school graduation, her dad even buying her a gorgeous corsage. They'd helped her move into her college dormitory, even paying her first year's tuition.

The weekly phone calls home were more dutiful than an excited sharing of her new life with them, and weekly became biweekly, then monthly, then only at holiday times.

This was especially true after she moved in with Mason. Her old-fashioned parents had been against her living with a boy without the benefit of marriage. At least wait until after graduation, they said. You've not known this boy that long.

Maybe they'd been right. Keira was prepared to admit this to them. She was prepared for a lot of things, throwing herself on their mercy. Eating humble pie would be tough, but she was out of options and this child growing within her depended on her.

That's what Keira told herself as she stood on their front porch. They were her parents. They'd raised her. They loved her. Yeah, she might have to listen to some lectures and bear their disapproving glances and disappointment, but they'd help her. She was their only child, of course they would.

Leaving her overnight pack propped up against the outside wall of the house, Keira knocked at the same time as she inserted her key in the lock, a lock she hadn't turned in over three years. This used to be the only home she'd ever known. What was the protocol for coming back? Did she knock and wait for them to open the door for her? Or did she do what she used to do and unlock the door and enter? She compromised by doing both at the same time.

Coming down the hallway was her mom. The woman's wary look gave way to sunshine, pure delight at the sight of her daughter. She offered outstretched arms, enfolding Keira into a tight embrace.

Grateful and uncomfortable at the same time, Keira stood awkwardly, unused to physical affection from her mother. From either of her parents; they weren't that type of family.

Heavier treads came down the hall, and over her mom's shoulder her dad approached. He stopped as his eyes met Keira's and a smile lit his face, crinkling his eyes at the corners. It wasn't quite a grin, because Bill Foster didn't do grins, but it was a smile - genuine and welcoming.

It would be all right. These were her parents, and they loved her. Keira relaxed, the dread in her heart lifting. "Hi, Dad."

"Our little girl's come for a visit. Come in, come. Maryanne, we need a fresh pot of coffee, and how about some of your carrot cake?"

Her mom fussed over getting Keira seated on the love seat, trotting back and forth from the kitchen as if she couldn't settle into making the coffee while her eyes needed to feast on her child.

The familiar scent of lemon furniture polish filled the room, even over the aroma of freshly ground coffee beans and percolating caffeine. The room was immaculate, not a speck of dust daring to roost near the doilies or coasters that covered every wooden surface. The creak of her dad's recliner as he eased his butt into the worn indentations, the place between the living room and kitchen doorway where the floorboard squeaked, even the same magazines arrayed on the shelf under the glass coffee table were the same. Only the dates had changed, the only evidence that time had marched on.

Well, that and the smiles on her parents' faces. Growing up, Keira had often felt part of the furniture - there, and accepted, but nothing special. Now, they saw her, really saw her, and liked what they saw. Keira relaxed into the familiar love seat, the place that was always her spot when they watched the evening news together.

Nursing his mug of fresh coffee, Bill said, "What brings you here today?"

Maryanne chirped in, "Oh, Bill, she doesn't need a reason to come home. We're just glad she's here."

"True, little girlie, true. You're a sight for sore eyes." He'd always been one for cliches. Growing up, Keira used to play in her mind the saying he'd bring up for every situation. She'd gotten better at the game over the years, predicting the correct one at least three-quarters of the time, by the time she left home. She'd probably have been more accurate, but she tired of the same old ones he'd used, and drummed up fresh ones in her mind. She knew these people well, the couple she'd lived with for 18 years.

"How's school? What's going on in your life?" Her mom still hadn't taken a sip of her coffee, never taking her eyes off the daughter who was back sitting in their living room.

Keira put down her cup, careful to place it in the center of a coaster. "Mom, Dad, I have a problem." She glanced between the two of them. "I need your help."

"Is it money?" Her dad leaned onto one hip, pulling out his wallet. "I imagine things get tight toward the end of your final year. How much do you need?"

Grateful at his willing generosity, Keira relaxed even more. Why had she been nervous? These people were her parents; they loved her and would support her.

"Yes, Dad, it's partly about money, but there's more."

Her dad ran his index finger along the edges of his wallet. A frown creased her mom's brow. "What is it, dear?" Maryanne asked.

There was no way to ease into this. Besides, that wasn't Keira's style. "I'm pregnant."

She'd read about what it was like being in the eye of a tornado, that place where the air changed, where a vacuum existed, sucking away all sense of sound and time. She waited in that void.

Maryanne recovered first. "Where's Mason?" She

glanced toward the door, as if she'd inadvertently left him standing there.

This was even harder. "He's gone."

"Gone?" her dad barked. "What do you mean, gone? Gone for the weekend? Gone fishing? What is 'gone'?"

"Gone as in he left when I told him." Keira's voice was low, both her parents straining to hear, but they did.

Tears trembled in her mother's eyes. "But he's coming back?" She said it like she wasn't sure if she was making a statement or a question.

Bill was on his feet. No tears for him. No, rage would be the way Keira would describe it. "You mean to say that this boy is not marrying you?"

Keira shook her head. Pretty hard to plan a wedding if the groom-to-be wouldn't even accept her calls. "No." Not that she'd want to marry a guy who reacted to life-changing news by running.

"Out!" Bill's outstretched arm pointed to the front door. "Out. Get out of my sight. Get out of our home."

She'd never seen her father's face like that, going from ruddy to almost purple. "But Dad…"

Beside her, Maryanne made little bird-like noises as she alternated squeezing the fingers of each hand with fist of the other. "Now, Bill…"

"Now, Bill, nothing," he roared. "She has disgraced us. This child we raised has turned her back on all that we taught her, all the values we hold high." More quietly now, "What a slap in the face. All the promise you showed, thrown out the window." He narrowed his eyes at Keira. "Get out of our house. You have betrayed us. From now on, you are dead to us. We have no daughter. We never want to see you again." In two strides, he was at his wife's side, helping her to her feet, leading her from the room.

The quiet weeping of an old woman, the rigid back of an old man, were the last glimpses Keira had of either of her parents. That is until today at the mall.

"Momma, Momma." Keira roused herself from her rumination. Daniel knelt beside her on the couch, both hands patting her cheeks, smearing the tears she had not known she shed.

She needed to get it together for him. Daniel's empathy could be way off the charts; he felt deeply and the look on his face told Keira that his mom had frightened him with her crying. She gathered him to her. "It's okay, son, it's okay. Mommy's okay. It's just a sad part of the movie." Sheesh. Had she actually lied to her child? Better that than let him in for the world of hurt if he ever learned how his grand-parents had reacted to news of his existence.

Daniel's skeptical regard said he wasn't fooled, but he settled down, snuggling into her side to watch the rest of the movie. It wasn't long before his breathing evened out and he slept, his weight a comforting burden in her arms. Resting her cheek on his head, Keira relaxed, letting go of the present and past burdens that had been weighing her down.

Chapter Eleven

Metallic sounds startled Keira, scraping coming from the front door. Before she could gently set Daniel aside and get to her feet, the front door opened and shut, admitting Jake. He locked the door behind him, slipping off his shoes.

"What are you doing here?" Walking into the hallway, Keira's voice betrayed traces of her nap.

"I thought I'd just show up." He held up his key. "I worried that if I called first, you'd make up an excuse why I shouldn't come over."

He was right, she probably would have. Like a magnet, his soft baritone voice drew her to him.

Jake studied her face as she approached, noted the traces of dried tears on her cheeks. Resentment he'd had over her rejection fled. "Come here," he instructed. "You look like you could use a hug."

Keira had no idea how long she stood there, melded into his embrace, his calloused hand brushing up and down her back, the pressure just right. This man had become her haven, so integral to her and to Daniel.

She stiffened, reliving that last day in her parent's living room. She'd vowed never to count on a man, never to lean on anyone else ever again. She'd be all that she and her baby needed.

How could she forget that so quickly? There was something alluring about Jake, something intoxicating that lowered her guard. She could not afford that. She had Daniel to think of, as well as her own heart. She pulled away from his warmth.

But he was having none of it. Loosening his arms for just an instant in response to her pressure, he pulled her back in, resting his chin on top of her head. "Not so fast. I need a bit more of this." Kissing her hair, he said softly, "I've missed you, you and Daniel."

As if on cue, there was a scrambling from the living room. Keira barely stepped back in time as Daniel launched himself with a gleeful, "Jake!" Jake caught the child in mid-air and held him like a monkey plastered to his chest, rocking from side to side.

Keira met his eyes, then looked away, avoiding the depth of emotion she read on his face. He was not making this easy.

"Come on, Daniel, it's bedtime."

Daniel allowed himself to be set down with one final hug. He didn't protest as his mom led him upstairs. It was late. Maybe they could skip a bath just this once. "There's charcuterie on the coffee table, if you want," she said over her shoulder as she guided her son up the stairs.

It didn't take long to get Daniel settled; he was half-asleep before she began his bedtime story. When she re-entered the living room, hostile eyes met hers. Jake stood in the middle of the room; papers clutched in his hand.

"What the hell, Keira?" He glanced from the sheaf of papers to Keira. "What's this about?"

She'd printed out flight itineraries with seats for two. She'd printed off lists of houses to rent, houses in Texas. Lots of tech companies had moved there from California and freelance work should be readily available. She hadn't meant for Jake to see these. She was just thinking, trying to work out her options.

"Nothing. I was just poking around, looking through some sites."

"Enough that you printed them off?" He looked again at the flight itineraries. "These tickets are for two people. *Two*, Keira. And they're one-way." He didn't come any closer, just looked at her. "Two." Jake stared at the empty air above Keira's head. "When were you planning to tell me about this?"

"There's nothing to tell. I have made no plans."

"Maybe not yet, but you're thinking about it." He clenched his hands. "What about me? How do I figure into these plans of yours?" Or do I even, he added under his breath.

Keira caught that last bit. Truthfully, when she had considered the possibility of moving, no, Jake had not figured into her plans. Her thoughts were solely on taking Daniel and running where Mason would never find them. But how to explain *that* to Jake?

"Are you saying we're done? Just like that, we're over and you're moving on? Geez, Keira, if I'd known that was why you were freezing me out these last few days, I'd have been over here immediately." He lowered his voice. Hurt and anger melded together, but getting mad at Keira would only push her farther away.

Warring with herself, Keira decided. He deserved to know her instinct to flee had nothing to do with him.

"I've been getting these calls."

Instantly, he was in front of her, grasping her by the upper arms. "You have a stalker?" The snake Alejandro came immediately to mind; he'd terrorized their friends over the last few years.

Keira shook her head. "No, nothing like that. Relax, Jake. I'm fine, we're fine."

Right, thought Jake. Fine enough that you're looking in to running away. Holding on to his patience, he waited.

"This was delivered by courier today." She handed over the papers from Mason and his lawyer.

Jake began reading, an expression of incredulity. His eyes darted to the signature. "Who the hell is Mason?"

Feigning calm, Keira took a seat on the sofa. "He's Daniel's father."

"How come I've never heard of him before?"

"Because he's not in our lives. Never has been."

It clicked. When they'd first started going out, Keira had told him how the father of her kid had ditched them as soon as he found out she was pregnant. Troll. "Then what's this about?"

"A week or so ago, I started getting calls and texts from an unknown number. I ignored them. But Daniel answered my phone one time and brought it to me. It was Mason. He said he wanted to meet Daniel."

"What did you say?"

"I hung up on him."

Jake rattled the papers. "Doesn't look like that was the end of it."

She shook her head. "He kept calling, saying he wanted Daniel, that he had rights."

"I'd say he gave up his rights when he walked out on you."

"Yeah, but he doesn't seem to think so."

"Why now? I mean, Daniel's seven years old. Where's the guy been all these years? Is he offering child support? Apologies?"

"No, well, sort of. He says he was a stupid kid then, and he's sorry, and that he wants Daniel now." The feisty Keira was back now. "He can't have him."

Jake pulled Keira to him, feeling her trembling.

"There's no way he can have him, can he?"

As much as Jake wanted to tell her no, he wasn't sure. "Let me read these papers." He went to Keira's desk, pulling open the top drawer to grab the pair of drugstore reading glasses she kept for him there. Since he only needed specs to read, he was constantly losing his pair. Not exactly *losing*, just misplacing them. For his last birthday, Keira bought him a dozen pair, squirrelling them away in all the places she'd seen him hunt for his glasses.

Normally, Jake hated having to don glasses to read. Brendan ribbed him about getting old. Usually, Keira joined in, but now didn't seem like the time poke fun at Jake. Leaning both fists on the desk, Jake levelled a gaze at his girlfriend. "I don't know what pisses me off more - the fact that some guy is trying to do this to you, the fact that you kept it from me, or that you were thinking of cutting out on me." Her desk chair creaked as he sat down hard. "Let me read this first, then we'll talk."

She kept quiet while he flipped through the pages, then started again at page one.

"He can't do this, can he? He can't make us do a paternity test?"

Removing his glasses, Jake rubbed his brow. "I know what you'd like me to say, and I'd love to tell you that no way. This is all bogus. But I'm not sure it is. Biological fathers have rights, even absentee ones. From what I gather, he's asking you to submit Daniel to a paternity test so prove whether this Mason character is the father."

"And if I refuse?"

"Then it sounds like he'll take it the next step and try to have a court order that you have to comply."

"Can they do that?"

"I don't know. Maybe. Next week when I run into one of the DAs at work, I'll ask them about this."

Keira tensed.

"Not about you and Daniel, sheesh Keira. Give me some credit. I won't mention any names. I'll just ask in general."

"Thanks. I'm a bit jumpy, I guess."

"Yeah, well, you and me, both. I just found out that my girlfriend considered running out on me."

"Jake…".

"Okay, okay. We'll leave that for now." He fixed her with a look. "But not forever. We're coming back to this."

She nodded. She'd hurt him. That had not been her intention; her aim was to protect her son. Everything receded into the background. But Jake need not be collateral damage.

Jake changed the subject. "Why now? Has this guy contacted you before?"

"Never."

"I wonder what's changed? So, what if a test proves he fathered Daniel? You said he wants to meet Daniel?"

Keira nodded again.

Jake pulled her back against his chest. "Well, who wouldn't? He's a neat kid." He settled them more comfortably into the couch cushions. "Maybe the guy has a guilty conscience and wants to make up for screwing up before."

Nope, that didn't sound like Mason, Keira thought. He only did things to serve his own purpose.

Chapter Twelve

On the other side of town

The plush, scarlet carpet muffled her steps. Annette Henry descended the curving staircase as Mason hung up his coat. "Did you do it?"

"Yeah, she should have it by now."

"So, by tomorrow, the lab should have the kid's DNA swab."

Mason wasn't as sure. "Maybe." The Keira he'd know a decade ago would have fallen in with anything he suggested. The one he spoke with on the phone now had little resemblance to the girl he'd once known.

"How can she not?" She fisted her hands at her side. "There's no choice. We need the proof that he's your kid."

"If she doesn't do what we want, then the lawyer will petition the court for a mandated paternity test." Sometimes Annette was a bit intense. "Don't sweat, it'll get done. It just might take a little longer."

"If she only knew how important this was. We've got a deadline to meet."

"Not sure that would help our case if she knew."

Chapter Thirteen

Abigail knocked on the drawing room door where Adele Henry sat knitting. "Excuse me, Mrs. Henry, but we have a problem. The Alpina is due for servicing today, but Oliver's sick. He could barely stand upright when he got out of bed, so I made him get right back in. He asked me to cancel the Alpina's appointment at the BMW dealership and reschedule."

"Nonsense. I'm sorry Oliver is ill, but I know how he looks after my cars for me. I can drive my own car to the appointment. Not a big deal. I've been there often enough, and they know me at the dealership. They'll do what they have to do. They'll bring me a latte and canape while I wait, then I'll come home."

Sure, it sounded fine, Easy peasy.

Getting there was fine and the coffee in the comfy lounge rich and creamy, along with the assortment of dainties on a china plate with a lace doily.

Then what was it? Boredom? A sudden urge? Maybe there was something compelling that needed doing somewhere nearby. This driving compulsion to move. She opened the door and stepped out the main doors of the dealership.

Outside, nothing looked familiar. There was this pressure, this urgency to be somewhere fast. Picking up the pace, her footsteps became faster and faster, too fast to notice the approaching curb. Then, she was on the ground, knees and shins stinging with scrapes from the concrete.

Cars whizzed by. A man pulled over and tried to talk. A stranger. Can't be too careful of strangers. Need to get away. Maybe he'd pushed her and caused the fall.

No idea where, just the urgency to go, to escape.

Finally, no one close by. Deep breath in. Okay, that man was not around. Time to figure this out.

Was it an appointment? Late for something? Images flitted by, like rapid camera shots, just as quickly floating away, replaced by something else, something that couldn't possibly be right.

The tree house Oliver built for Annette when she was just a little girl. Her husband, Hubert and her, skiing at Vail, long before Annette came into their lives.

Why these things? Why now? They had nothing to do with the present, but images of past times continued to flood in. That combined with the awful urgency, the need to keep going and going.

Tired. These old bones were tired, legs not used to walking so far. Felt like hours and hours on her feet.

This was ridiculous, of course it was. Stop and figure it out.

Okay, got it. The BMW dealership. Car. Servicing.

That's it. Everyone knows what a Beamer sign looks like. Just scan the area, find the sign, then walk to it.

Can't. Like a dream, a nightmare impossible to escape. Know it's a dream, of course it is, half awake, knowing it's not time to get up yet, but if you sink back into sleep, the trap of the stupid dream will seize you again and you're powerless to stop it.

Ah, there it is, the BMW sign. Relief, an immense burden, lifted.

Then, it wasn't there. Holes, holes in time.

A residential area, a poorer neighborhood. Sidewalks crumbling, tree roots pushing up through the concrete, lawns uncut, and yards unkempt.

Flailing. Unable to stop the fall. Knee of pants torn and tattered.

Up ahead, on the corner. A store, a convenience store. Yes!

Heading to it, a car came out of nowhere. The driver honked and slammed on his brakes, yelling out the window. His words made no sense, but the menace in his tone clear.

Back up, back up, away from him, from the angry man. Heels backed right into the curb, butt contacting the sidewalk, hard. Palms scraped in a futile effort to break the fall.

Lights, colored lights hanging from poles in the air. They meant something, of course they did. But what? Figure this out. Stop? Go? What?

Another break in time, then the convenience store.

Inside it was so bright, the fluorescent lights such a contrast to the fading sunlight outside. The lights hummed and one flickered in a most annoying manner. Why didn't someone fix it?

Music playing, that modern stuff where they talk to the

beat, rather than sing. Loud! So loud! Impossible to think over all the racket.

Too much, too much. Get out, flee to some place calmer.

Ow! Who put that stand of chocolate bars right in the middle of the aisle? Now they were all over the ground. Impossible not to crunch them underfoot.

Yelling. A young man yelling something about "Get out" and "drunks".

Time. Had that just happened in the store, or was it hours ago? Years ago? Where was Annette? Was it her bedtime? She'd need a bedtime story. Who would tuck her in? Gotta get home.

Streets, so many streets.

Trees. Branches reaching over the sidewalk, black in the dusk, like tentacles bending down, trying to grasp unsuspecting pedestrians. Brushing branches let loose showers of water droplets.

Rain. It hardly rains in San Diego, but when it does.... The heavens open up. Torrents of rain, causing hair to hang like rat's tails in the face.

Dark, so dark. Where had the day gone?

A stoop, someone's house. An older house, run down. The rain gutter unattached along the side of the house, and hanging down. Oliver needs to have that fixed.

The doorknob turned easily, no entranceway, just directly accessing the living room.

A woman entered and started screaming, "Who are you? What do you want? Get out, get out!"

Yeah, good idea. But how? Yes, escape this raving woman, but how? Feet with no ability to back up or turn around. Oh, so complicated.

Can't speak. Can't move. Can't get away from this screaming woman.

Then the woman stopped and stared, but her stares were worse, piercing right into the soul. She started talking, moving her lips, but her sounds made no sense.

Closer and closer she came, slowly, like approaching a wounded animal. Her mouth kept moving, but it was impossible to hear her words, to make sense of them over this black, roaring cloud filling all the mind's corners, every single crevasse.

Then she was there, right there, right beside her, too close, close enough to touch.

With a sudden lunge, the woman grabbed the purse off my arm, then backed away to the other side of the room. She stuck her hand right inside the purse, bringing out a cell phone. *Her* cell phone. Had it been there all along?

The woman started looking through the phone.

Mason was always saying to password protect that phone. But that would require tapping in a damned password every time she wanted to use the stupid thing. Another thing to remember. Not happening. Passwords were the bane of existence. *Everything* required a password these days, and they wanted you to change them all the time, too.

The odd word came through now. Something about the letter A. Then contacts, then Abigail. Abigail. That sounded right, some elusive tendril hard to grasp.

The woman put the phone to her ear and started talking. Her words rippled around the room, swirling, sometimes touching down to make sense, most often not.

A knock on the door, a sharp rapping. "This is the San Diego Police Department. Open up. We received a call about a disturbance."

Chapter Fourteen

Adele Henry picked up the phone. It was an old-fashioned, black plastic one attached to a landline, much preferable to those tiny cell phones. Sure, she owned a cell and knew how to use it, or at least she used to.

Adele relied on muscle memory to dial the number. It worked this time, although even that kind of recall was not something she could rely on anymore.

She spoke as soon as Missy picked the call up. "It happened again."

"Oh, no, Adele. I'm so sorry. Are you all right?" Missy Tait, her best friend for over 60 years, didn't need an explanation. "I'll be right over."

Some of the adrenalin-infused tension left Adele's 71-year-old body. Growing old was definitely not for the weak. That was especially true when your aging body had few people to rely on. Sure, there were Abigail and Oliver Norris, her housekeeper and butler. She trusted them as much as possible, but their relations were of employer and employees. Not the same as someone who stuck with you because they loved you, not because you paid for their services.

But Missy, she was different. They both grew up on this estate, Adele the daughter of the owners, Missy as the only child of the cook, living with her mom in a carriage house beside the estate.

With Missy, there were no pretenses, no need to sustain the facade of a woman in control of all she surveyed, including her faculties.

The door chimes echoed through the marble entryway. Adele heard the murmur of voices as Abigail, the house-keeper, invited Missy inside.

Hearing voices, Annette and Mason emerged from the sunroom, drinks in hand. As usual.

"Gram, what are you doing here?" Mason came forward to give his grandmother a hug. After his dad's desertion, Missy had taken him and his mother into her home, caring for both of them until his mom ran off in search of more exciting company than that of an old woman and a small boy.

Annette waited for her turn, kissing the air near Missy's left ear, giving a hug without actually making physical contact, all without spilling a drop of the gold liquid in her old-fashioned glass.

The girl left Missy cold, but her grandson seemed enam-ored with her. So, she'd be polite, both for his sake, and for the sake of her old friend, Adele. After all, Annette was Adele's granddaughter, and her only remaining relative. Although the more she worried about Adele, the harder Missy found it to make nice to her friend's granddaughter.

From her vantage point around the drawing room door,

Adele watched the interaction. Ah, she knew Missy well, noted the slight stiffening of her shoulders at Annette's approach. Even Missy's closed eyes didn't hide her distaste.

She doubted Annette noticed and if she did, she wouldn't care. Annette lived in a reality of her own making. As long as she got what she wanted, the pesky details didn't matter, especially those concerning other people.

But that was Annette; she was what she was.

And, if she had less than admirable traits, well, who was there to blame but Adele? She'd raised the child. Even when the no-good parents were around, they'd left Annette's care to a nanny and Adele. Then they'd gotten themselves killed by an avalanche while helicopter skiing while the child was still a toddler.

And now, almost thirty years later, they were in this mess.

Missy entered the drawing room, pulling tight the pocket doors that would block their conversation from both their grandchildren and the staff.

Missy knew this would not be good when she saw Adele had already poured them each a tumbler of The King's Ginger. This was their go-to comfort drink when things were tough, through marital trials, when the weight of rearing grandchildren seemed too much, through physical maladies, and more recently, mental tribulations.

"Tell me," Missy directed.

Cradling her glass with both hands, Adele eased into it. "The Alpina was due for its servicing yesterday."

Missy took a sip, allowing Adele to stall, if she needed to. Oliver, the butler and chauffeur, took good care of all of Adele's cars, but his joy was the BMW 7 Alpina.

"Oliver was sick." At Missy's raised eyebrows, she

nodded. "Yeah, I know. It hardly ever happens. He tried to get out of bed, but could hardly stand, Abigail says. She made him climb right back in, then came to tell me he'd not be able to work today. He asked her to cancel the Alpina's appointment."

Ah, Missy could see where this was going.

"I told her nonsense. I could drive my own car to the appointment. Not a big deal. I've been there often enough, and they know me. They'll do what they have to do. They'll bring me a latte and canapé while I wait, then I'll come home."

"Right." But Missy knew it hadn't worked that way. "But…"

"I don't know what happened. I got there just fine and was enjoying my coffee in the lounge." That troubled look came over her face. "Then, I don't know. Maybe I got bored. Maybe I thought of something I needed to do at someplace nearby."

Missy thought her friend looked like a smaller version of herself. An older, tired version.

Adele paused, composing herself. She felt that sensation of panic building once again, threatening to overcome her. No, she needed to finish this. Missy needed to know the true extent of what was happening to Adele's mind. She'd never survive without Missy's help.

From Missy's expression, Adele knew that she'd gone away for a while there. These periods of absence, of losing track of where she was in a conversation, were happening alarmingly often.

"One minute I was enjoying a latte and goodies at the BMW dealership. Then next thing I knew, I was standing outside my front door, with a police officer on either side of me. The door opened and Abigail stood there, a shocked look on her face."

Missy waited.

"Before that, I guess I went into someone's house and the woman there called the police. While she waited for them to arrive, she grabbed my cell phone."

"Ah, good, you had your cell with you."

"Sure, it would have been good if I'd remembered I had it, or how to use it."

Oh, poor Adele, her intelligent, competent friend, able to handle any situation, until this.

"I guess the woman called Abigail. Abigail is the first person listed in my contacts, so she was ready when the police brought me home."

"What did she tell them?"

"She made excuses and said we'd be in the next day to explain. I guess the officers could see that they weren't getting any sense out of me that night."

"The next thing I remember is being upstairs in my bedroom, with Abigail saying she'd poured my bath and to come get in."

"You seem fine now."

"Yes, I do. I'm me again."

"What did you tell Abigail?"

"Nothing. What could I say? She's a wonderful employee, always circumspect. My torn clothes are gone, and she made no comments about my appearance, or where the car was."

"Do you think it's time to bring Abigail and Oliver into this?"

"I think I'll have to tell them at least some of it."

"You can trust them?"

"Trust them not to tell Annette? Missy, they don't like her any better than you do."

Missy blushed and didn't meet her friend's eyes.

"It's all right. I don't like her either most days, but she's all I've got. If that ridiculous will wasn't ironclad, things would be different. As it is, our plan is the best thing we can do to make things right."

Chapter Fifteen

Missy drove an impeccably groomed Adele to the police station. This was Adele at her finest, Adele the woman who commanded respect when she entered a room. Gone without a trace was the disheveled, frail, confused old woman the police had picked up the night before.

Of course, it was not the same officers on duty, the ones who witnessed Adele at her worst moments.

"Good thing you had your purse with you, Ma'am. Your wallet had your ID with your address."

Taking charge, Adele showed them the letter from her neurologist stating her diagnosis and that it was a progressive dementia.

"Do you not have a Medic Alert bracelet?" Office Podantz asked.

"What is that?"

"My grandmother has Alzheimer's, and we got one for her. It's an engraved bracelet that lets emergency service staff know to contact Medic Alert for her information.

Pertinent medical or cognitive information can be shared almost immediately."

Missy took notes. "We'll contact them immediately."

"The other thing we did for my grandma was to have information throughout her house, info for *her*. Sometimes she would get confused and not know who she was or where she was. So, these index cards taped to walls, and in drawers she often used, listed her name, the name and number of a family member to call, and stuff like that. She's used it a few times. In the back of all her coats, my mom sewed a label with her name and a contact number, in case she got lost and someone found her. Little things like that make us feel better."

Podantz's partner had some paperwork ready. "If you'd like, I can register you with us. We keep a file for vulnerable persons who might be found wandering. Totally your choice, but it's a safety service we offer."

Never was Missy prouder of her friend as Adele maintained her dignity as she posed for a photo ID picture, filled out the required documents and submitted to the indignities of what was actually being publicly declared incompetent.

"There's just one other thing," the policeman said without meeting their eyes. "We had a call from a convenience store early yesterday evening. The employee reported a woman entering the store, flailing around, and knocking over a stand of chocolate bars before taking off." He cleared his throat. "According to the store's security tapes, I believe you were that person. I'm pretty sure they'd be willing to drop any charges if they were compensated for the ruined products and display stand."

Money. Thank goodness money could hide a world of ills.

Annette had spent the day at a spa, chilling. Now they relaxed in the theatre room of Adele's house. "Looks like you didn't know your old girlfriend as well as you thought you did."

Mason tried not to wince at the venom in Annette's voice.

The DVD was just over, an old one, *Fatal Attraction*. Annette had a unique spin on the ancient flick. She thought Alex was misunderstood, only doing what she needed to do to get what she thought she was owed. Annette loved such films and often had unusual takes on antagonists.

Initially, that had been part of her appeal. Annette was not your run-of-the-mill girl, but her own person. Mason, often blown by the winds of whatever was popular at the moment, gravitated to someone like Annette, someone who knew her own mind, someone who went after what she wanted.

And Mason was what she wanted, apparently, although he suspected their grandmothers had a hand in them getting together.

Mason and Annette knew each other as kids; of course, they did, with their grandmothers being best friends. The old ladies had brought their grandkids for play dates, likely more of an excuse for them to hang out together than for the benefit of the kids. Still, Mason never minded roaming around the enormous estate, and Annette always had fun games up her sleeve, things Mason would never have thought of on his own. He was positive his gran had no inkling of half the stuff they got up to. Oliver did, though, as he was generally the one who discovered their mischief.

But he mostly hid it from the grandmothers, cleaning up after their mishaps with just an admonition.

Now that Mason was living in this house, Oliver showed him the respect due to the partner of the future mistress of this place. As it should be.

"Mason!"

"Ah, sorry." Annette didn't like to be ignored. Hated it, in fact. She had no patience for when Mason would get lost in his head. No, she deserved full attention and demanded it.

"So, you're doing it tomorrow?"

As they left the 12-seat theatre room and headed for their private wing of the house, Mason reviewed the last words he could remember Annette saying. Oh, yeah. Keira. Damn her, she'd ignored his note. "Yeah, tomorrow morning I'll phone the lawyer and tell him to submit the court petition. It's all ready." Mason had been less confident than when he told Annette that Keira would comply with the paternity test. He'd been franker when alone with the lawyer, and had the papers drawn up just in case they needed a judge to enforce the DNA test.

"Do you think she'd get with the program faster if we hinted that there might be something in it for her?"

No, Mason didn't. In fact, he was pretty sure it might blow up in their faces.

"We wouldn't actually have to follow through with giving her anything."

"We'll try it my way first." Sometimes a man had to at least pretend he was in charge.

Chapter Sixteen

They waited until Daniel was in bed to talk about this. Keira searched Jake's face. "It's not good, is it?"

He shook his head. "I'd like to tell you what you want to hear, but the DA wasn't hopeful. She said that the biological father has the right to know if a child is his. You can submit the cheek swab to the lab as requested or wait until it's court ordered. If this Mason guy carries it that far, the DA was almost positive a judge would uphold his request."

Keira masked fear with anger; it was a trait she'd had to develop. "And if I don't?"

"Don't shoot the messenger. The DA said that the test isn't difficult, just a cheek swab. If you do it yourself, and send it into the lab, that's all you have to do. If you wait for a court order, then the chain of evidence must remain intact. You no longer get to do the swab, but a stranger would have to do it, probably at the lab itself."

They shared a look. A stranger touching Daniel, sticking something into his mouth? Taking him to some lab that might smell funny?

Keira liked neither option. "What if I don't? What if I don't do either thing?"

Jake knew what she meant, back to the plan of running. "They'll find you, Keira. This crosses state lines." Plus, her running would not work for him, not one bit.

Keira turned away, staring out the window into her backyard.

Nope, she was not shoving him away, not this time. He wrapped his arms around her shoulders, relieved when she leaned back into him. "We're in this together," he reassured her.

Keira tilted her head to look at him.

"I love that little boy, too, you know. I love him as much as if he was mine. In fact, I hope that one day I'll have the right to call him mine." He felt her stiffen and pull away. "I'm not trying to scare you. That can be a discussion for later. For now, know that you're not alone. We both have what's best for Daniel as our aim."

"I know you care about him. He loves you, too."

Yeah, Jake knew that, and it warmed his heart. For a single guy who'd never thought much about kids, he couldn't believe how a little boy had wormed his way into Jake's heart. Although he knew this wouldn't sit well with Keira, he needed to say it, anyway. For Daniel's sake. He turned her to face him. "If it's inevitable that Daniel will have to submit to a paternity test, maybe it's better to do it now. Do it here at home with just you and me present. Daniel won't think it's a big deal, especially if we pretend to do it to ourselves, too." This would be less scary than going to some lab and having a stranger use the swab.

"So, what if we did this? What if we do the DNA test and it says in writing that Mason is the father? I already know that. What difference could it make?"

Ah, that was the problem. "The DA said that sometimes these tests are done to prove paternity so that a father is forced to pay child support."

"I don't want anything from him."

"I get that." Here was the hard part. "She said that sometimes even absentee fathers have a change of heart and now want to be part of their child's life." There. He'd said it.

Keira pulled away, her eyes blazing. "But he can't! He made his choice long ago. He didn't want us, so fine, we managed on our own. Daniel is mine and mine alone. Mason can't have any part of him."

The courts might see it that way. There was a chance.

Chapter Seventeen

It was here. The subpoena giving Keira a court date to appear regarding a paternity test.

Putting it out of her mind, trying to lose herself in work and in playing with Daniel hadn't made it all go away. Mason was determined, she saw that now.

Keira called Jake. "I should have listened to you. It's going to happen anyway, whether or not I ignore it."

She didn't have to explain what she meant. It had preyed on Jake's mind, too.

Keira continued. "Can we stop it? What if I did the swab at home, right now, and took it to the lab? Could we halt the court proceedings?"

"Yeah, I think so. I'll check with the DA and call you back." Now that he was off the phone, he could not stop the grin that spread across his face. She'd said we - not I, but we. She was including Jake in this. At least something positive had come from all this worry.

Jake skipped lunch so he could bank the time and take off early to be at Keira's when Daniel arrived home from school. They'd take the swab, then Jake would swing by the lab to drop off the sample. Unfortunately, a copy of the results would need to go to Mason as well if they wanted to halt the court's involvement. Since they didn't have Mason's mailing address and Keira was loath to contact him, they gave the address of the lawyer's firm from the original paternity test request.

"I don't know why I'm so nervous," Keira said. It's not like I don't already know Mason is the father. "It's wondering what he might do with that knowledge that keeps me up at night."

Less than a week later, Mason's lawyer requested he come in for an appointment. Annette insisted she accompany him, certain that she could move things forward better than if she left Mason to do it alone.

"Mr. Cooper, do I have your permission to speak freely in the presence of Ms. Henry?" He didn't look pleased that Mason had brought along his girlfriend.

"Yes."

"Very well. Ms. Foster complied with the request for DNA testing. I have contacted the court to withdraw the subpoena now that the results are in."

Annette edged forward in her seat.

"They analyzed twenty loci on the DNA samples provided by both you and by the minor, Daniel Foster." He looked up from the lab report. "I've made a copy for you, and you can go through it, if that's your wish. But the bottom line is the Combined Paternity Index. It says that there is over a 99% chance that you are the biological father of this child."

"Yes!" Annette threw an arm around Mason's neck.

Ignoring the young woman's obvious glee, the lawyer continued. "Of course, we can dispute this if you wish. There is no chain of evidence with this and, while it's clear that you fathered the child whose sample was analyzed, we have no guarantee that child was in actuality Daniel. Do you wish to dispute this?"

Mason shook his head. "No, the results are exactly what I wanted, what I thought."

The lawyer looked between Mason and Annette. "You look like you have a plan."

"Yes." Calmer now, Annette continued. "We want his son. Mason's been without the boy for too long and wants to change all that now."

The lawyer's eyes shifted to Mason, his client. "What do *you* want?"

"Annette's right. We're settling down and want a family. I already have a child and he'll make our family complete." He checked with Annette, as if asking if he did good.

"The boy already has a mother he lives with and has been with all of his life." What were these two up to?

"Oh, we know that," said Annette. "And we're grateful to her for looking after him up to now. But we have so much more to offer the child."

"This is your plan?" The attorney needed to be clear about this. "You want to take the child from his mother and raise him yourselves?"

Mason nodded.

"And you think the mother will agree to this?"

"Of course," Annette said. "Once she sees the life we

can give Dennis, compared to what she as a struggling, single mother can offer, it'll be a no brainer."

"Daniel," corrected Mason.

"What?" Annette turned to him.

"My son's name is Daniel, not Dennis."

"Oh, yeah. Whatever."

"If you aren't sure of his name, I take it you don't know this child well."

Studying his nails, Mason explained, "Actually, we've never met him."

Interesting. "Maybe start with that. Have you talked with the mother about meeting your son?"

Mason fidgeted with his phone. "Yeah, a few weeks ago."

"And?"

"She said no." Actually, it had been more than a simple no, more than a hell, no, even.

"But she can't refuse now." Annette was confident of this. "Now that we have proof he's Mason's son, Mason has rights."

"True, he has some rights. I'd suggest you talk to the mother again, requesting to meet the boy. If she still refuses, then we have some legal recourse, although it will take time."

"Time?" Annette's voice rose. "We don't have time. How long will this take?"

It had been over seven years since the child's birth. What was the rush now with these two? "Why don't you start with meeting your son." They might change their minds after that.

Chapter Eighteen

After getting the paternity confirmation results, Keira and Jake sat up late that night discussing possibilities.

Maybe Mason developed a conscience and remorse for abandoning his girlfriend and child all those years ago. Maybe his intentions were innocent. Maybe not.

It wouldn't hurt to get a lawyer, someone who knew the ins of outs of paternity and custody stuff, someone on *her* side, on Daniel's side.

Anna. Their friend, Anna, would know. Anna was a social worker, often performing court-appointed interventions in child custody disputes. She'd know a lawyer sensitive to the needs of a child like Daniel and his mother.

Although she said she could do it alone, Keira was glad of Jake's company at this initial visit with the lawyer. Jake had lots of banked overtime he could take and insisted he come too. Of course, she knew he could not insist on anything when it came to her or Daniel. Even so, it was nice to feel his hand in hers.

It had been an education, even before this first appointment. Keira had thought the terms lawyer and attorney were interchangeable. Not so, Anna informed her. Anyone finishing law school and passing the bar exam was a lawyer. The term attorney was short-form for attorney-at-law, a lawyer who can also practice law in the courtroom. Anna thought it was safest that Keira work with an attorney just in case things escalated to the courtroom.

So, an attorney it was.

Ms. Julie Franco was the attorney Anna recommended, and when Anna called her, opened up a slot. So here they were.

It didn't take long to bring Julie up to date. There wasn't a lot to say - absolutely nothing for almost eight years, then a flurry of calls or letters these past two weeks.

With Keira's permission, Julie's secretary made copies of the previous letter from Mason, from Mason's attorney, as well as the DNA results.

She relieved Keira's mind when she applauded her decision to go ahead with the DNA test prior to being ordered to do so by the Court. "You're showing that you're a reasonable person."

"I don't care if I'm reasonable or not. My goal is to protect my son. That's what matters, not what Mason thinks of me."

"I agree. Your son's best interests are what matters." Julie folded her hands and leaned forward. "However, what you feel are your son's best interests may be differ from what his father feels." She waited for a heartbeat. "Or what the Court believes."

"What do you mean?"

"You, understandably, have a low opinion of the father of your child. He deserted you, both of you. But biological parents have rights, no matter their past behavior."

As Keira protested, held up her hand. "Oh, there are exceptions, of course. If the father has a history of misbehavior toward minors, or sexual or physical abuse, etc. We'll look into this," she checked her notes, "this Mason Cooper to see if he has any such history. But, barring that, he most likely has a right to meet his son, to have contact with him. If his history is clean, I would be surprised if a Court did not uphold Mason's claim to rights to Daniel."

"Rights?" This came from Jake.

"Rights could mean anything from the occasional visit, to shared custody, to even a petition for full custody."

Keira was on her feet. "No! No f'ing way."

"Please have a seat, Ms. Foster. It's my job to be honest with you, to lay out all eventualities. I'm not saying it will go that way, or even might. Given Mason's lack of interest in the child for the past decade, it's hard to imagine he's suddenly dying to be a father figure."

"But? I hear a but coming," muttered Jake.

"It won't help if you're not cognizant of how this could play out. For now, I think you need to be tactical. You've taken a good first step with the DNA testing. The next step is to have Daniel meet his dad." She waited for the storm she knew would come. "Under your direction, of course. I'd suggest that you pick a day, time and place, then invite this Mason to meet his son. And you'll be present, naturally."

Deflated, Keira sank back into her seat. She felt about as old as her son. "Do I have to?"

Jake took her hand. "It looks that way. I'm sorry you have to go through this. I'll be right with you every step of the way and protecting Daniel will be our goal." He directed his hardest stare at the attorney in front of him. "Right?"

She could not bear to speak with him in person. Just the thought of allowing that man into her home made her skin crawl. But she'd do this, do it for Daniel.

She sent a text:

> If you still want to meet your son, be here between 3:00 and 4:00 on Saturday afternoon. The date and time are non-negotiable.

Looking at the message before sending it, Keira reluctantly erased the last sentence. There. That was about as grown up as she could get. She hit the button that would send that fifteen-word text over the airwaves, a message that could change their lives.

It seemed only seconds before a reply came.

> Great! We'll be there Saturday at 3. Can't wait to meet the little guy.

We? No! There was no "we". It was enough that she'd have to tolerate Mason. But no one else. Who was this "we" anyway? No, who cares? No, just no. Quickly, she typed.

> No! Just you. That's enough for Daniel.

The response took longer this time.

> Ok. I get it. Just me. This time.

Chapter Nineteen

Mason parked Annette's Maserati at the curb in front of Keira's house. Even if it wasn't his, it was still a cool car to drive. Obviously, fellow motorists thought so too, from the envious glances he received.

Once old Adele kicked the bucket, all of her cars would be Annette's, would be *theirs*. While this Maz screamed flash, he preferred the elegance of the Beamers. Maybe he'd take over the Alpina. His hand brushed the creamy black leather of the seat beside him. Nice, but not as nice as that of the Alpina. Things like the wood on the dashboard, small touches that made a difference. It was the little things in life...

Dragging his gaze from the car's interior to the yard outside the passenger window, he told himself he needed to assess the place, learn as much as he could about Keira and her current life in order to help move their plan forward. He was not, definitely *not*, sitting here because he was nervous about meeting his son.

The front curtain twitched. Busted. She knew he was here.

Mason exited the car, carefully to press the door shut, not slam it. A car like this deserved respect, even if Annette treated it casually. Rubbing his palms on his thighs, he strode to the door, wrapping confidence around him like a cloak. Fake it 'til ya make it...

He had to knock twice before the door opened. Then there she was. The first girl he'd loved. The first one he'd ever thought of as more than a fling. Keira. "God, you're beautiful." The words burst out of him before his brain even registered that they'd formed.

A man came into the entryway and put his arm around Keira's waist. "Yes, she is."

Mason took a half-step back toward the door he'd just entered. Could the guy's brows get any lower? It was never a good sign when a man scowled at you like that. He held up his hands, palm out. "Whoa. No offence. Just making a statement." He checked Keira out. "You've aged well since I last saw you."

As Jake took a step forward, Keira's arm held him back. "You're not here to chat, Mason, or relive old times. Those were not good times, by the way. The only positive coming out of knowing you was Daniel." She crossed her arms. "Still determined to meet him, or should we say goodbye?"

Over her shoulder, Mason spied a freckled face with deep red hair peeping around the corner. It was like paging through Gran's old photo albums. No, there was no need for a DNA test to prove that his genes lived in that boy's body.

Following his glance, Jake looked toward the living room. "Come here, bud." He held out his arm.

The small boy hastened from where he lurked, over to

Jake's side, wrapping his arms around the man's legs, as Jake's arm automatically sheltered Daniel, cradling the child's head to his side.

"Let's go into the living room." Keira led the way. "Daniel, this man would like to meet you."

Daniel turned his face into Jake's side.

Jake knelt beside the boy. "It's okay, bud." He turned the child in his arms until he faced Mason.

"Daniel," Keira said, "this is Mason. He's a… friend." The word stuck in her craw.

Mason bent his knees, bringing his face closer to the level of the child's. Spreading his palms on his thighs, he gave a quick look at Keira, not missing her hesitation at the use of the word 'friend'. "Hey, little man. I'm Mason. How are you?"

Daniel studied the stranger's face for a few seconds, then stuck out his hand.

Accepting the handshake, Mason gave a half-smile at Keira. "I see the kid has manners."

Daniel freed his hand from the man's grasp, and returned to his blocks on the floor, his duty done.

So, what's the protocol for meeting your son for the first time? Lowering himself to the ground, he hoped no one heard his knee pop. "Ah, are you going to leave us alone?"

Keira shook her head.

"Not on your life," Jake muttered.

Okay, that's how they wanted to play it. This was no worse than that elective drama class he took at college. He could perform in front of an audience. It was a tad uncomfortable to have them standing, looming over him. He'd connect over Lego; every kid loved Lego, even though it had been over two decades since he'd touched the stuff. "Hey, what are you building?"

Silence.

Maybe the kid was shy. "Can you show me what you're working on?"

Without his eyes leaving the pile of bricks on the carpet, Daniel held up the partially built vehicle, shoving it closer to the man.

Taking the creation, Mason spun the front wheels. "Nice. What goes on the back here?"

Again, silence.

Mason looked at Keira. If she'd teach the kid to shake hands, surely, she taught him how to make polite conversation, or at least to answer a simple question.

She returned his gaze.

He tried again. "Want me to help you build this?"

With a quick shake of his head, Daniel took back the car, then turned his shoulder toward Mason.

The kid might not want to speak to him, but his message was clear. Rising to his knees, Mason asked Keira, "Is the kid shy?"

"Not especially."

Another thought struck. "Can he talk?" Sheesh, the kid, was seven. When did kids begin talking, like maybe around two or something?

"Some."

What? What the heck? What is 'some' supposed to mean. "Does he talk or not?"

"A bit. He communicates in other ways."

Yeah, Mason got the message that the kid didn't welcome his intervention in the Lego department. How could a kid this age not talk? "Is there something wrong with him?"

"Absolutely not." This came from Jake. Then, as a reminder, "He can hear everything you're saying."

"There's got to be something going on if a kid this age doesn't speak." No, since he'd come through the door, he was certain he'd not heard a word from the kid's mouth. He got to his feet. "Is he, like, simple-minded? I don't know the politically correct thing to call it these days. Retarded?"

Keira's face whitened, then tightened.

The anger on Jake's was easier to read. Jake stepped forward, one hand a clamp around Mason's upper arm. "That's it. We've had enough of you. This visit is over."

Not until Mason was deposited outside on the porch did the vise-like grip on his arm loosen. The guy stepped back into the house; the house containing *his* son and *his* old girlfriend. Mason heard the sound of the lock, then the deadbolt closing, shutting him out.

Annette was in the rooftop hot tub when Mason returned home, her favorite spot. Accessible only by a curving, stone staircase spiralling up the inside of a turret, then opening to an expansive patio space with incredible views. Annette raised her glass of Prosecco in greeting. "How did it go?"

How'd it go? Good question. "Well, I met him."

"And?"

"There was no need for a paternity test. He's the image of me at that age." At least physically, that is.

Annette's stare recognized there was more to this.

"There's something wrong with him." Gotta be. "The kid didn't say one word the whole time I was there."

"Maybe he was overwhelmed. Shy. It's not every day a father drops into your house, someone you've never met before."

"They didn't introduce me as his father."

Annette quirked a brow.

"Just as a friend." Yeah, that irked. "But they didn't act like it was odd that the kid didn't speak. I asked if there was something wrong with him, but they denied it."

"Is he retarded?"

"They threw me out when I asked."

"They?"

"Keira had her boyfriend hanging around."

Annette sipped her sparkling water. "I'll check with Grandmother, but I don't think the Will said that any kid had to be in his right mind, just be a part of the family." She peered at Mason over the gold-wrapped rim of her flute. "He'll do." Setting her glass on the side of the hot tub, she sank low in the water, submerged up to her chin. "Doesn't matter if he's an imbecile, or a gimp, or purple. As long as he's a kid, and *our* kid, he'll do."

Some wiggling and maneuvering, then her hand emerged from the steamy, frothing water, waving her bikini bottom in the air. "Coming in?"

Chapter Twenty

Julie Franco's receptionist left a message, requesting that Keira come to the attorney's office for a meeting.

"Maybe she wants to tell me Mason's backed off. Meeting Daniel once was enough." Hope filled her eyes. "Maybe this is all over."

Jake hated to burst her bubble. "Do you really think so?"

Her shoulders sagged. "No. I don't."

"When shall we go?"

Grateful for his support, she dialed the office.

Seated in the brown leather chairs across from Julie's massive desk, Keira clutched Jake's hand. "Good news?"

"Depends. Mr. Cooper's lawyer says it pleased his client that you gave him access to your son. He complains the visit was brief, but not inappropriate for an initial meeting."

"It was short because he acted like an ass in front of Daniel. Talked about the kid as if he wasn't sitting right there in front of him." It still ticked Jake off the things

Mason said. Some father. Instincts of a gnat and that was an insult to all gnats everywhere.

Julie picked up the papers in front of her. "Mr. Cooper is requesting increased access to the child."

"What's that mean?" Keira didn't know if she could sit through another visit from Mason.

"Generally, that means longer visits, visits away from your home, without you being present." She pressed on despite the alarm on Keira's face. "Overnight visits with Daniel in Mason's home, then longer times when they are together."

Keira was on her feet. "No! No way. Leave that man alone with my son? Never! You didn't hear how he talked about Daniel. No, just no."

Jake stood beside Keira, his arm around her shoulders, his stance echoing what Keira had just said.

"Please sit down, Ms. Foster and Mr. Dean. I realize this is alarming to you."

"Damned right it is!"

"We have an issue here." Julie paused to find the right words. "I get that you don't want this man around your son. But he's the father; the paternity test proves that. As such, he has rights."

"How could he have any rights? He deserted us. He wanted no part of either me or the baby. He's ignored us for seven years, then thinks he can come waltzing back into our lives as if none of that mattered. No, that's just wrong."

"I understand how you must feel. But the law is on Mr. Cooper's side. As the father, he has the right to see his son, be a part of his life."

"Is there no way around this? I'm a cop, and I've known parents who were not allowed anywhere near their kids."

"Do either of you know anything about Mr. Cooper's

personal life? His past?" Julie looked hopeful for the first time since Keira and Jake entered her office. "Has he ever been convicted of pedophilia? Of child abuse? Does he have a history of violence?"

Keira shook her head. "I haven't heard from the guy in over eight years. No idea what he's been up to during that time, but I doubt he'd any of those things you mentioned. Surely, I'd have noticed evidence of his being assaultive, or any of that." She turned to Jake. "Is there a way you can find out?"

Julie intervened. "Rather than put Mr. Dean in an awkward position of possibly accessing databanks illegally, why don't you leave this to me. I'll put my people on it and we'll unearth any sign that Mr. Cooper has indulged in practices that would warrant banning his access to his son. Will you leave this with me?"

It was a week before Julie requested Keira return to her office. No, there was nothing in Mason's background that would preclude him seeing Daniel, the attorney explained. "Therefore, we should proceed with plans for Mr. Cooper to spend time with his son."

"No. I said no last week, and my decision hasn't changed. It will never change." The feisty Keira was front and center.

"I'm afraid that this is out of your hands, Ms. Foster. There are just two ways this can go. One, we can work this out between us and Mr. Cooper's lawyer. That way you'll have some input into times, dates, maybe even places."

Keira's head swivelled from side to side.

"The other way this could unfold is through the Courts. Given his clean background check, I can't see the Court denying Mr. Cooper's request to spend increasing time with his child."

"But he can't. He didn't want Daniel. You can't just change your mind about a thing like that."

"I'm sorry, but he can, and he has. You can lay out a schedule of visits, suggesting places and times, or you can let the judge determine those things." Julie studied the tightness of Keira's shoulders. "You might not like the result. The judge might order shared custody."

That did it. "I'm out of here. I'll get Daniel and we'll go." Keira started for the door.

Jake caught her hand and pulled her back. "No, Keira. You're not running. You could make things worse."

"Mr. Dean is right," Julie assured them. "Flight would be the worst thing you could do now. Leaving the area, leaving the state with a minor child would not go well for you. You'd be found. Custody could even be awarded to the birth father, with *your* access to Daniel limited."

Jake pulled Keira in close, wrapping in his embrace. "We'll get through this. We'll protect Daniel," he whispered.

"Is there any other reason Daniel should not see his father?"

Keira raised her head. "There might be one thing…"

Chapter Twenty-One

Three Weeks Ago

"Are we doing the right thing?" Missy was less sure.

"We've been round this every which way. I don't like it, either, but can't see any other way of making this happen." Adele had made many decisions in her life, none as momentous as this.

"Look at us," Missy said. "Two old biddies manipulating the future."

"Well, our kids haven't left us much choice."

Both women contemplated their offspring. Missy's daughter had trailed after a singer in a band. Regular groupie, she was. Proximity and persistence paid off and finally Stan the Man had noticed Sue - noticed her enough to get her pregnant. But at least he stuck around, even marrying Sue, in a quick elopement. In a moment of maturity, he told Missy that he wanted Sue and the baby cared for if anything happened to him. Confidence, he had, and belief that his music career would skyrocket.

There was a blaze, yes, but it was a blaze of fire when his truck careened off an overpass. The band members following in their bus talked of the substances Stan had taken that evening.

Despite Stan's statement about looking after his young family, he didn't. There was no money either in his accounts, or in any sort of insurance policy. Maybe he would have hit it big, maybe he wouldn't have. Moot point now.

Despondent, Sue had spent the rest of her pregnancy at home with Missy, content to be waited upon. Missy got it, really she did. She'd had a rough time when carrying Sue, so knew the fatigue involved with nurturing a new life. But unlike Sue, Missy had worked through all but the last few weeks of her pregnancy. Had to.

Once the baby made his appearance, Missy knew, just knew, that Sue would come around. Maybe this responsibility was just what her daughter needed to become an adult.

Hadn't happened. The demands of the babe overwhelmed Sue, relying more and more on Missy for the daily care. He was a good child and slept through the night within a few months. Life would get easier. As far as kids go, Mason wasn't difficult to manage. He met all the expected milestones, even if it was Missy who took him for his checkups and for his baby shots. It meant she had to take time off work to get him to these appointments. She tried to encourage Sue to at least come with them, but no, she was too wrapped up in her soaps and other afternoon shows to budge from the house.

Then she did budge. One day, Missy came home from work to the wails of a child. A child alone in the house, a child who'd tried to get himself something to eat, emptying cereal boxes all over the floor, a child with a diaper reeking enough to water the eyes of the toughest earth mother.

That was the last either of them had heard of Sue.

Funny how it had turned out. Adele had been her best friend since childhood. It was Adele who stood by her through those harried days of looking after both her adult child and that child's baby. It was Adele who hired private investigators to search out Sue's whereabouts. It was also Adele who convinced Missy to give it up. Dragging Sue back from her latest groupie fling would bring no joy into any of their lives.

Yes, Adele was the strong one, but even her mettle was tested with her own son.

Jason was, well, how to describe him. Missy loved him. Of course she did. He was the child of her best friend, after all. Plus, who was she to criticize? While her own daughter had her head in the clouds, her feet never quite touching solid earth, Jason's head and fingers craved baser things, things money could buy. He grew up with wealth; it had been in his family for generations, that much was obvious. What he didn't see was the way his parents had taken those inheritances and made them grow. To Jason, money was a means to an end, a way to get what he wanted. And he wanted lots.

It was at college that Jason met Rachel. Both students enrolled in classes, rarely completing them. No, that wasn't quite fair. Rachel had completed two years of college, mostly successfully, before she met Jason. Then the fun began. What was the point in slaving away at the books, when Jason's fingers dripped the funds to do anything they wanted?

The birth of baby Annette barely slowed down those two. With Grandma Adele and nannies around, hands-on parenting was a plebeian task neither Rachel nor Jason need bother with. The world abounded with adventures just waiting for them.

A ski trip ended in disaster when the helicopter they'd hired to land atop a mountain trail triggered an avalanche. There were no survivors.

So, both Adele and Missy raised their grandchildren.

The two children knew one another as kids. Despite Annette being two years younger, Mason followed her around during their play dates.

With Annette away at boarding school in her teen years and Mason attending the local high school, they lost touch. A chance meeting brought the two back together. Well, that and their grandmothers.

At first, Missy and Adele laughed about it, commented on getting old and forgetful, both of them. That stuff happened to everyone.

But Missy started noticing other things about Adele, worrisome things. The always confident, always in control Adele periodically seemed confused. It was not just losing track of their conversation, but she'd suddenly stop in her own house, looking around as if she didn't know where she was. Ridiculous, since she'd lived there for well over four decades. Still, that aura of bewilderment would come over Adele's face and she'd need Missy to guide her out of the room, away from prying eyes. Sometimes the fog cleared in a few minutes, sometimes a few hours.

It got worse.

The diagnosis was frontotemporal dementia, a form of pre-senile dementia. They learned that pre-senile dementia was when this degenerative disease came on before the age of 65. Even people as young as 40 got this, so it wasn't out of the question for it to affect a 70 year old, even if Adele didn't *feel* old.

Cells in the temporal and frontal areas of the brain are lost, causing these areas of the brain to shrink. As they found out, the frontal and temporal areas of the brain were important to everyday living. They involve memory, emotions, reasoning, and planning. Disruptions in these areas can bring about changes in the person's movements, personality, behavior and the ability to manage day-to-day affairs.

Earlier, these were merely annoyances, brief flashes of what she and Adele liked to call brain farts. They laughed about them. But even three years ago, Missy could see the fear in Adele's eyes, even though she tried to hide it.

For someone in Adele's position, these deficits were miti-gated by her wealth. She had employees to do things like the cooking, cleaning, yard work and household chores. Oliver doubled as chauffeur, butler and managed the permanent and seasonal staff.

But there was the future to think about.

You never stopped being a parent; they agreed about that. Or grandparent.

Adele worried about Annette. Of course she did. Annette, for all her smarts, had little idea about how life worked. Surrounded by money all her life, she expected it as her due. Except, without Adele, that cushion of wealth would vanish overnight.

Adele's deceased husband's ancestors believed in family. After one wayward son had burned through a fortune, the rest of the relatives circled the wagons. Never again would money be handed down to a wastrel. Only family men would be in charge of the finances, or women, if there was no male heir.

This section of the family was down to just Adele and Annette. Adele feared her days were numbered, and the neurologists backed this up. Second and third opinions differed only slightly in their guesses at a timeline. The outcome of frontotemporal dementia was certain. Adele would lose more and more ability to manage her own affairs and the progress of the disease would speed up as her brain suffered increased damage. Death would follow.

Without Adele around, Annette would have access to only a paltry sum of money, not enough to support her needs for even a year. Unless, and there was a big unless. If Annette was married and had a family, the terms of her father's will would be met, and the full inheritance would be hers.

The catch was, Annette wasn't married and had shown no moves in that direction. So she needed a push.

Adele and Missy conspired. Both their grandchildren needed stability. Neither was inclined to work, facts that pained their grandmothers' hearts. After all, who had raised these young people? Who had instilled in them the values that would fortify them in life? The two old women feared they had failed their offspring in this area.

But there was one last thing they could do. Annette and Mason needed financial security; heaven knew they'd not be able to create it on their own.

A child might plant their feet on the ground, give them a sense of responsibility or purpose. Or at least one could hope. And hope was all Missy and Adele had left.

Although Mason had been living with Annette in her

wing of Adele's house for over a year, they produced no child. Two healthy young people with at least some modicum of libido should have created at least the spark of the next generation. But no, nothing.

The time for subtleties passed. The only decision was how much to disclose?

Chapter Twenty-Two

They figured it out, with the help of the lawyer, who had served Adele's husband well. There was nothing in the terms of the will stating that the marriage had to be a love match, just legal and with offspring. If the current heir died or became incapacitated, the Estate would pass on to the next in line, as long as the marriage and family conditions were met.

Since they didn't know how much time Adele had left physically or mentally, they needed to put this into the laps of their grandchildren fast. That meeting had been almost a month ago.

"Hey, Gran." Mason had kissed Missy's cheek. "What's this about?"

"Have a seat, please." Adele pointed to the couch. "Annette, you too, besides Mason."

Annette slouched, bored. Well, thought Adele, that was about to change.

"I'm old," she started.

Annette gave a snort.

Mason nudged his girlfriend, casting a hasty glance at his grandmother, his cheeks slightly reddened.

Good, at least the boy has some of the manners Missy taught him. "Obvious, isn't it?" She addressed Annette. "When you get old, you think about the shortness of life."

Annette rolled her eyes and reached for the ever-present glass of an adult beverage.

"I'm telling you this, Annette, because it will affect you." It was obvious her granddaughter paid more attention to the swirl of the ice cubes in her drink than to Adele. "If I die, there is no money."

That caused Annette to sit up.

"Your great, great grandfather made a will, one that abides to this day and stands after my passing." She paused to make sure Annette let these words penetrate. "Our family money can only be inherited by a direct descendent."

Annette relaxed.

Adele continued. "Not just any descendent, but that person must be married, with a family."

The corner of Annette's mouth turned up in a sneer. "How stupid is that? Archaic. Get the lawyer to change it." She dismissed her grandmother, getting up to leave the room.

"Sit down!" Although she didn't raise her voice, the steel was evident, even to Annette. "The will is iron clad. When I die, you will inherit nothing, that is unless you are married, with a child."

Adele looked at Missy, who gave a nod. Adele turned to Mason. "That's where you come in. You might have wondered about your grandmother and I orchestrating you and Annette meeting again, and might have even felt like we were throwing you together."

In truth, Mason hadn't noticed. He just went with the

flow, and living in a mansion had more perks than he could count.

Missy took over. "Mason, you know we are not wealthy. When I die, you'll get my house and car, but little else. There just is no money." She sighed. "I know you got your degree, but I also know that you're not into working for a living." More shame on her.

"I never said that," sputtered Mason. "I've had jobs. I'm just in between them now, waiting for the right opportunity to come along."

"If you're with Annette, working for a living will be optional." Adele assessed the impact of her words. "That is, if you're married to each other, and have a child."

Annette and Mason exchanged a look.

"I take it you're not opposed to having sex? With each other?"

"Geez, Gran."

"Well, boy that's what it's going to take, that and some nuptials if you want to help this little girl secure her fortune and help yourself in the process."

Mason took Annette's hand as they walked up the curving staircase that led to Annette's wing of the mansion.

Part-way up, Annette pulled her hand free. "Race ya," she said.

From her vantage spot near the drawing room door, Adele shook her head. Annette never changed. Life was always a game, a challenge to her, even as a child. Now, Annette still turned things into a competition, even with her boyfriend.

Mason trod more sedately behind Annette, content to

follow. Believing them alone, he opened the topic simmering between them. "Awkward, wasn't it?"

"A bit out of my comfort zone," agreed Annette.

"Never thought we'd be discussing our sex life with our grandmothers." Pulling closed the double doors to their suite, Mason turned to Annette, resting his back against the thick panelling. "What are we going to do?"

"I'm certainly not going to tell Grandmother about my botched abortion."

Botched was right. The ensuing infection led to Asherman's Syndrome and permanent scarring. Asherman's would have been treatable if attended to back then. But Annette had been busy; doctoring was low on her list of priorities when she was no longer pregnant. But it left Annette unable to conceive, or at least the doctors gave her something less than a one percent chance. So what, she'd thought? She'd never cared much for kids, anyway. There was too much to do in life than to spend precious hours cleaning snotty noses, or worse.

Now, though, now it mattered. Unless she could produce a kid, she was screwed out of a heap on money.

"Adoption?" asked Mason.

"No, that takes years. Grandmother is old, already in her 70s. Who knows if we'd be able to adopt a kid in time?" She kicked off her shoes. "Guess we better try, though." She gave him her best bat-your-eyes-smile. "Would you look into that tomorrow for me?" She knew he would. He'd do anything she asked, always had.

"Sure." Something tweaked a synapse in Mason's brain, one he'd tried to dampen each time it fired into action. "Ah, I might have another idea."

"If it's getting me knocked up, I'm not opposed to

trying, but it's never worked with anyone in the last dozen years."

"I'm game to try." He grinned at the woman reclining on the king-sized bed. "If adoption's okay, and it doesn't have to be a child you gave birth to, then there might be another way." He pulled off his shoes and socks and crawled onto the bed beside Annette.

"Years ago," he started, "just after I finished college, I was living with this girl. She got pregnant."

Annette sat up in bed. "What happened to the kid?" This might work.

"I dunno. I took off. I was scared, and no way did I want to be a father. I was just starting my career, beginning to get some decent money coming in."

"Anything like *my* money?" She needed to keep him dangling close by.

"Nowhere near your money."

"Do you think she aborted it?"

Mason shook his head. "I doubt it, not the girl I knew. Besides, I think she said something about it being too late in the pregnancy."

"Ah. She tried to trap you. Smart man to get away."

"No, I don't think so. That wasn't Keira's style."

"Where is she now?"

Mason shrugged. "Maybe we'd better find out."

And they had. Keira hadn't been that hard to find, not when she hadn't changed her name and worked in the same discipline she'd been studying when they'd been in college.

"Got her!" Annette was pumped. "Now to get your son."

So began the texts and phone calls.

Chapter Twenty-Three

Awkward. Mason sat on the floor of Keira's living room, his back against the couch, legs spread out wide. Thank God, he had his phone, otherwise he'd die of boredom.

In the corner, Keira sat at her desk, working on her computer. Near him, but not too close, Daniel fit together the pieces of a jigsaw puzzle.

He'd need to get the kid some better puzzles if that's how he liked to spend his time. Daniel'd brought this huge Ziploc bag with all sorts of puzzle pieces of color and size, some with ragged, torn edges. Couldn't Keira afford new puzzles for the kid? Ones that stayed in their own boxes?

Mason used his phone to go online to Amazon, searched out puzzles appropriate for seven-year-olds, and ordered half a dozen. They'd keep the kid quiet, giving him something to do when he came to Annette's and Mason's place.

While he'd concentrated on his phone, the heap of puzzle pieces by Daniel changed shape. Some now attached themselves to finished pictures. The kid didn't organize the bits by size, shape of color; instead, he just reached into the pile, withdrawing the piece he sought, fitting it into the puzzle he worked on. How'd he do that?

Boooring. How long was he supposed to sit here? Checking his watch, only 20 minutes had passed since he entered this house. An hour, the lawyer told him - make the next few visits about an hour in length as his son got to know him.

Yeah, well, like that was happening. Only the left side of Daniel's face was visible from where Mason lounged.

Keira. You'd think she could help him out here. But no, she, too, ignored him. "Hey," he called to her. "Do you have to keep working over there? Doncha wanna visit a bit, catch up on old times?" Anything to kill the boredom.

Cool eyes turned from the computer monitor to Mason's face. "Yes, I have to keep working here. This is how I support us, my son and I."

Ouch.

She continued. "And no, I have no interest in catching up with you. Even less interest than you showed in us for all these years." Keira glanced at Daniel and bit her lip.

"Well, I'm here now. That oughta count for something." Was that an eye roll he caught, an actual eye roll? Yeah, there was some of the Keira of old still there, buried under this frosty exterior.

One word interrupted their interchange.

"Jake?" This came from Daniel.

"What?" The first word Mason had heard from the kid's mouth, and it had to be *that* guy's name.

"Jake?" Daniel asked again.

"Jake's at work. He'll be over after supper." Keira returned her attention to her screen.

"He talks?" Mason asked.

Keira's glare almost wished he hadn't spoken, but he needed to know. "The kid can talk?"

Keira's eyes flicked between Mason and her son, their son. "I told you, explained to you. Did you look up any of the stuff I told you to read?" She did something with her hands, then looked at him expectantly. "Did you learn any of the signs I showed you?"

A shrug. "I've been busy." Yeah, they both knew he didn't have a job, but what she didn't understand were the demands on his time. Annette was a high maintenance gal, commanding effort and focus. And it was all worthwhile for the lifestyle, the life he'd be able to give his son. He didn't have time to read the boring stuff she gave him. Something about *Autism Questions Parents Ask*.

Daniel shifted on the floor, his back now to his father.

How could he have agreed to Annette dropping him off here, leaving him stranded at Keira's house without a way to escape?

Time dragged.

Having completed his puzzles, all eight of them, Daniel left them spread on the floor. Stepping over Mason's legs as if they were part of the furniture, Daniel picked up the remote control, turned the television on and brought up YouTube.

He didn't know a lot about parenting, but there were some pretty iffy things on YouTube. Should Keira be letting the kid do this? She appeared not to notice. Maybe she wasn't the perfect parent after all. He stored that info away; might come in useful sometime.

The kid seemed to know what he was doing. Soon the screen filled with the most amazing Lego creations ever.

Daniel settled himself on the couch, one sneakered foot clipping Mason on the side of the head. The kid didn't seem to notice.

Mason rubbed his ear to ease the slight stinging. Soon, the screen captured his attention. A kid's toy or not, this was actually interesting. Maybe he and his son were finally bonding.

The doorbell startled all of them.

Keira got up from her desk and checked the peephole in the door. A woman about her own age stood there, shifting her weight from foot to foot. Annette. She matched the picture Mason had shown her and Daniel. She unlocked and opened the door.

With a smile ready to crack her face, Annette entered, hand outstretched. "Keira! I'm so happy to meet you!"

Keira took a step back, away from this effusive woman. Reflexively, she offered her hand.

Annette grabbed it in both of hers, not letting go. "Hi! I'm Annette, Mason's fiancé." She released Keira's hand but stepped in closer. "Give me a hug." She wrapped her arms around Keira's shoulders or tried to. "I've been so wanting to meet you. I feel like we're sisters, bonded by Mason and dear little Dennis."

"Daniel," Mason's voice said from the living room doorway. "His name is Daniel, not Dennis."

"Oh, silly me." Annette beamed. Little details didn't matter. "Where is the darling?"

Glancing at the couch, Mason saw Daniel hadn't

moved, still intent on studying the latest Lego build shown on the television screen.

Keira planted herself between Annette and her son.

With swift strides, Annette covered the distance between herself and Mason, turning her face up to his. "Give me a smooch, babe."

Leaning down, Mason gave her a chaste kiss.

Annette was having none of it. One arm coiled around his neck, the other hand resting on his chest. Bringing his head to hers, she gave a cinematic-worthy kiss, holding Mason in place.

It took both hands on her shoulders to move her back enough to sever their lip contact.

Annette ended it with a "hmmm," and a self-satisfied smirk. "Nice," she said. Then she placed a fingertip on Mason's lips. "More of that later. Promise?" From the corner of one eye, she checked if Keira watched.

Mason reddened slightly. This felt like high school and staking claims.

"Oh! This must be the little darling." Annette sped to the couch, sitting down beside Daniel, so close that she was almost on top of him.

Daniel scrambled away, clutching the remote.

"Oh, are you shy, little man? Come to mama."

Daniel scrambled off the couch and hid behind his mother.

The annoyed look showed through before Annette quickly masked it. "I'd expect better of you," she told Keira. "If I'm to be this child's mother, you should pave the way. It'll be easier on him if you do."

Mason stepped between the women. This wasn't the way, playing their hand too soon. "Annette, he's a child. Give him time to warm up to you." And to me.

With one hand protecting the child cringing behind her, Keira said. "I think you'd better leave."

Annette crouched to peek behind Keira. "Bye-bye, little man. We'll see you next week."

Chapter Twenty-Four

Little changed over Mason's next few visits. Daniel
continued to play on his own. After letting him in the door,
Keira ignored him, worked on her computer, with the occasional comment to Daniel when he'd bring a toy or creation
to show her. Mason, well, he had his phone for company.

Annette breezed in at the start and the end of these
visits, too busy to stay, brushing air kisses toward both Keira
and Daniel. At least she got the kid's name right now,
mostly.

Daniel ignored her, other than pulling away whenever
she came too close, bringing with her a cloud of perfume.

One small thing changed on the third visit. The puzzles
he'd ordered from Amazon arrived, so Mason brought
along two of them. With two 200-piece puzzles, maybe this
would give them something to do together.

After presenting them to the kid, Keira prompted her
son. "What do you say, Daniel?"

"Thank you," the child murmured, not meeting
Mason's eyes. He took the boxes, making quick work of the

cellophane wrappings. Opening the first box, he dumped the contents on the floor. Then he opened the second box, adding those pieces atop of the pile from the first box.

"Hey," Mason complained. He looked at Keira. Hadn't she taught the kid how to handle jigsaw puzzles?

Keira shrugged, then return to her work.

"That's not how you do it." Too late - the kid had already dumped them all together. Now it would be impossible to do with all 400 pieces in a jumble. Well, not his fault. He returned to the Facebook stream on his phone. Maybe at least some of his friends were doing something interesting.

Silence ruled in the room. Maybe not the companionable silence of a true family, but at least it wasn't combative. From time-to-time, Daniel moved from the floor to the other side of the coffee table. Whatever. It kept the kid busy. Finally glancing up, Mason noticed the picture taking shape on the coffee table. He picked up the puzzle lid. Holy cow, the kid was doing it. He was actually creating the puzzle, not even looking at the picture of the finished product. What kind of a brain could do that?

"You sure you're okay alone with him?"

"Sheesh, Keira. What do you think could go wrong? You'll be upstairs. If I need you, I'll yell." What kind of dork did she take him for? "Go do your conference call thing. We'll be fine here."

"Here's the social story I made for you. Be sure to go over it with Daniel several times at least. You can't just take him somewhere, especially somewhere like Chuck E. Cheese. You need to prepare him ahead of time, or it won't go well."

"Come on, Keira. Give me some credit. It's a restaurant meant for kids; he'll love it."

The next visit was different, their first actual outing. This one had been a battle between the lawyers, Mason's and Annette's wanting to push forward their involvement in Daniel's life, Keira pushing back, wanting things under her control.

She'd lost.

Chapter Twenty-Five

Daniel

Chuck E. Cheese, mom said. The man and the stinky lady were taking him to Chuck E. Cheese.

Mom said the lady wasn't stinky, really. She just had a heavy hand with perfume. Her hands didn't look especially heavy to Daniel. Didn't matter anyway - she still stank.

Kids at school talked about Chuck E. Cheese. They went there for birthdays and treat days. Funny that mom never took him there. But today was the day.

The man, Mason, rang the bell. Jake let him in, and the scent of the stinky lady's perfume made it through the entrance before she did. Mom was wrong. This was nothing like when she overdid the bubble bath. This was a stink. How could she stand to move around in a fog of the stuff? Maybe she had a stuffed-up nose.

"All set to go to Chuck E. Cheese?" the man, Mason, asked.

A nod, but wasn't it obvious? He stood by the door wearing his shoes and jacket. Sometimes adults didn't have a clue. And this guy talked all the time, seemed to need to say the obvious.

Mom ushered the lady back out of the house fast. Maybe she couldn't stand that smell, either. Jake held the door for us but didn't come. They still had only socks on their feet. What? Weren't they coming? No! They couldn't expect him to go with just these strangers. Even seeing Chuck E. Cheese was not worth it.

Resisting the tug of the man's hand, he tried to get back into the house.

"No, bud. You're having an outing with Mason and Annette this afternoon." Jake didn't look happy about it, though, and mom looked like she might cry.

No, something was going on. This was just wrong.

"Mason, grab the kid and let's go. We have a reservation, and I can't hang around all day." The stinky lady sounded mad.

"Jake, please…" Mom's voice wavered.

Jake squatted down. "Look, bud. You're going with these people to Chuck E. Cheese. That sounds like fun, doesn't it?"

Yeah, maybe.

"It won't be for long," Jake continued, "then they'll bring you right back here where your mom and me will be waiting."

No. This was definitely wrong. He went places with Mom and Jake, not with these other people. He hardly knew them, and one of them stank. Besides, they didn't even know basic sign language. Mom tried to teach the man, but he didn't get it. Nope, not worth it, even to see Chuck E. Cheese.

Jake reached out and gathered him into his arms. "Trust me, Daniel, it'll be all right. Just get in their car nicely. Don't make this any harder on your mother."

What?

Then Jake was at the door of a low car, opening the back door and placing him on a booster seat. Oh, yuk! It smelled in here, smelled of that lady and her stinky perfume.

The lady got into the car behind the steering wheel, bringing with her even more of that stench. She turned around with a smile that showed too many teeth. "We're going to have such fun!"

Then Jake gave a hug, shut the door and the lady pulled away from the curb.

Trying to follow the twists and turns of the route became impossible. How would he get home if he got lost? And the smell in the enclosed space made it hard to think.

But there was something good about this car. The seats felt so good, cool, and soft, making fingers glide along them. Over and over, he rubbed his hand along the soothing seat.

"Ew, would you look at that?" In the rear-view mirror, the lady's eyes met his. "Mason, the kid's rubbing his grubby hand all over the seat. I'll have to get Oliver to clean the mess off the leather."

Mess? What mess? The seat looked fine, just the way it had before. And grubby? No, mom made him wash his hands before these people came.

There were lots of cars in the parking lot where they stopped. The guy, Mason, got out of the car, opened the back door, and undid the seat belt on the booster seat, just like he was a little kid and couldn't do it himself. But the hand on his shoulder felt good as they walked to the Chuck E. Cheese entrance.

Did the lady never stop talking? Her incessant chatter on top of her stink made it hard to think. This was all new, and he needed to process what was going on around him.

The lady only went in so far, then stopped. Daniel didn't notice and plowed into her, putting out his hands to steady himself, his head full of the tinny speakers and some man yelling, "Make some noise for Chuck E. Cheese!" From another speaker to the side, a man in a wobbly voice sang, "With a little love, and some tenderness... with some peace and some harmony..." Peace?

The lady whirled around. "Watch where you're going!" She looked down at her white skirt. "And keep your grimy paws off me." Grimy? Paws? He didn't have paws, not like Amy's dog, Blitz. There weren't any dogs or cats here, not that he could see. And he'd *washed* his hands.

"We have to wait our turn," Mason said. "We have a reservation, but the place is full and our table's not ready yet."

Different kinds of music sprouted from various corners of the building. There were pings and beeps from machines, squcals from kids, loud voices of mothers and fathers calling to kids. Lights and colors flashed, and no one kept still. Colors and motion everywhere in a blur.

Grease. Yeah, that was in the air. And the aroma of pizza, maybe good pizza, but not with that grease, old grease.

Humming helped to stop the cacophony of input, except as the bombardment got louder, so did the need to hum and make noises to try to drown it out. Rocking helped a bit, too.

The stinky lady came close, throwing her scent over top of everything else. She was too close, and her leg brushed against his side. "Stop making that racket," she said, with a mean look on her face. "Stop it right now before you embarrass us any worse." Turning to the man, she said, "He's acting like a freak. Can't you make him stop? Can't you at least control your kid?"

More rocking. Harder. It was building. It was too much, all too much. The sounds, the lights, the smells, the confusion, and it was too new, and his mom wasn't here.

And then she was.

Suddenly he was hoisted high into arms, arms he knew. Jake's.

"It's all right, bud. I've got you. Your mom and I are here. You're all right now. We'll take you home."

The hand rubbing in circles on his back was his mom's.

It was okay now. He let himself go limp against Jake's side.

Back at home, it was quiet. Settled. Everything where it's supposed to be, including Mom and Jake. A bath helped, as did the macaroni and cheese. Comfort food, Mom called it.

As he half-dozed in front of the television, he listened to their conversation, going over everything again and again, like adults did.

"I should never have trusted that idiot to read the social story with Daniel. I bet he never did it at all."

"And they could at least have chosen a time when the

place wouldn't be so busy." Jake shook his head. "Even *I* was overwhelmed by the mass confusion of the place."

"It was the right thing to do to follow them, just to see if everything was all right." Keira shuddered to think what might have happened if they'd not shown up to rescue Daniel.

"What will the lawyers say about this?"

Chapter Twenty-Six

"Mrs. Tait? This is Abigail from the Henry residence. I wonder…" Her voice trailed off.

"What is it, Abigail? Is Adele all right?" Missy dreaded these calls.

"Physically. She's here, in the house, but this is not a good morning for her. So far, I've kept her away from the others, but…"

"I understand. I'll be right there. Just keep her in her own wing."

"What happened?" Missy arrived within fifteen minutes.

"She came down the stairs with her dress on backwards and unzipped." Abigail's feet shifted from side to side, and she didn't meet Missy's eyes. "It's happened before where she's come downstairs not properly dressed, but never this bad. And her hair stuck up all over the place."

They both knew Adele's pride in impeccable grooming.

"There's more." Abigail's guilt at ratting out her

employer sat hard on her heart. But she'd promised. "She tried to put on makeup but got it all over her face." Like a horror movie caricature of a clown.

Squeezing the woman's hand, Missy tried to reassure her. "You're not being disloyal. You're doing exactly what she asked you to do. Remember that. Together, we'll do what we need to do to protect her."

It had been a tough meeting. Adele and Missy waited until they knew Annette and Mason would be out of the house for a few hours.

"Abigail, would you call Oliver and the two of you meet us in the drawing room, please?" Not a usual request, but not unheard of, either. The last time had been to let them know that not only Annette, but her boyfriend, Mason, would join the household. A mixed blessing. Sure, company for Adele was good, rather than rattling around alone in this sprawling mansion. Mason proved easy to work for; less so, Annette.

In various capacities, Abigail had worked in the employ of the Henrys for decades, first helping with the cleaning, then in the kitchen until for the past ten years, she'd been in charge of all housekeeping and kitchen staff. Not that it took that many people to look after one old lady, but just keeping a place this size clean took a crew, even if most were just part-time.

Oliver, too. He'd started as a teen with a summer job working on the grounds. That's how he and Abigail met. Between the two of them, they now ran the place. Their duties were about to increase.

"Abigail, Oliver, please close the door behind you. I want this conversation to be kept between just the four of us." Adele inclined her head to include Missy. "I need to tell you about the terms of my will."

"Oh, Missus. We don't need to know things like that." They were close, but not *that* close. Plus, Miss Annette would hate that the servants had knowledge of the family's personal affairs.

As if Abigail hadn't spoken, Adele continued. "First, upon my death, the carriage house and two acres of the land it sits on goes to the two of you. Between my attorney and Missy here, who is the executor of my estate, the deed will transition to you smoothly."

Abigail and her husband exchanged glances. They'd lived there rent-free as part of their salaries since shortly after their marriage and had raised their children there.

"I don't know what to say." Oliver spoke for both of them.

"There will also be an allowance to look after the upkeep of the place until your deaths." Adele cleared her throat. "There will also be a wage increase for you both to cover the additional duties I'm asking you to take on." She looked at these people who were important in her life. "The title to the carriage house, though, is not contingent on your agreement to do what I'm asking next. Is that clear?"

Abigail and Oliver nodded.

"I'm ill." Adele knew of no easy way to get through this. "How long I'll live is uncertain."

Oh, no. She didn't *look* sick. "Anything we can do to help, we certainly will."

"That's what I'm hoping, although I know this is a lot to ask." Adele's voice cracked, and she looked to Missy for help.

"Let me try to explain," said Missy. "Adele has a diagnosis of FTD, frontotemporal dementia."

"Now, Missus," began Oliver. "We're all getting older, and our memories don't quite pull up facts the way they used to."

"Thanks, Oliver." Adele appreciated the effort. "True, but what's happening to me goes far beyond the normal effects of aging."

"We've been to a number of neurologists, and all give the same diagnosis." Missy looked at her old friend. "FTD it is, and when we research the subject, we find that yes, she has most of the symptoms."

"What can be done about it?" Surely something will help, and with the Missus' wealth, she can afford anything.

"There's no cure. And there are no medications to reverse or stop it, although some meds may help with the behavioral changes." Missy let that sink in.

"Behavior?" Oliver asked.

Adele again looked to Missy to explain. "Remember the other week when you were sick and Adele took the Alpina in for servicing, but you had to pick up the car the next day?"

"Yes, that was unusual."

"Unusual is one way to put it," said Adele. "I think you can expect lots more odd things from me."

Abigail frowned.

"Behavior changes are the norm with FTD," Missy explained. "They include, of course, memory but can also affect language ability - both in understanding what is said, and in speaking." She looked at Adele. "That's happened to Adele a number of times now. The worst was when she was at the BMW dealership."

They might as well know the full story. "I took off," said Adele. "I've no reason I left the building. One minute I was sitting in the lounge, enjoying a latte, the next I was wandering around outside, with no clue how I got there, or how to get back."

"Did your memory then just come to you?" Surely, this was the case. Maybe just a momentary blip in the Missus's mind.

"No," said Adele. "I must have covered several miles and ended up in some woman's house. The woman took my phone and dialed the last number from my recent calls list. Luckily, that was you, Abigail." As if saying this much, or the memories of that day exhausted her, Adele looked to Missy.

"You must have noticed her state, although she was coming out of it. We appreciate your discretion, not wanting anyone else to see the shape she was in. The next day, we went to see her neurologist. He said things like this would happen more and more often and we need to prepare."

"That's where you come in," said Adele. "That is, if you're willing."

Abigail's thoughts mirrored those of her husband. "Certainly, anything."

"First, don't let me drive. No matter what I say to you, don't."

That could get tricky. "What if you tell Oliver to give you the keys?" No way did Abigail want her husband getting fired.

Missy handed Abigail an envelope. "It's all in here. This is drawn up by Adele's attorney, explaining things. You can't be fired, at least not by Adele."

Adele nodded. "Missy now has power of attorney over me. We started out with Durable Power of Attorney, meaning she'd take over if I became incapacitated for any reason." She looked directly at her trusted employee,

Abigail. "And I am assured that I will become incapacitated. Then, after that episode, more MRIs, and a letter from the neurologist, it was time we had the DPOA changed to General Power of Attorney. So, it's done."

"What does that mean?" asked Oliver.

"Missy now has full control over all my legal, health, financial, and business matters. That's what I meant when I said that you could not be fired for not complying with what I ask."

Abigail and Oliver shared a glance. "How can we help?"

As if this hadn't been bad enough, now they needed to get into really personal matters.

"Annette."

Abigail knew this was coming.

"I don't want Annette knowing about my condition."

Missy covered Adele's hand with hers. "That's how you can help. Adele wants to keep this from Annette as long as possible. She thinks, and I agree, that Annette will not be happy with me holding Power of Attorney. After all, that affects the running of this household, and the allowance Annette receives."

Refraining from spilling anything to Annette was not a problem. Abigail avoided talking to her, other than when absolutely necessary.

"I've given each of you a 20% raise." Noticing their looks, Adele explained. "That was *before* I gave Missy POW, and my attorney witnessed it, so it's for sure. You'll notice the increase on your next pay checks. That's for your trouble." Adele sighed. "And I know that I'll be creating trouble for you over the next while, making your jobs harder."

"Not at all, Missus."

"That's nice of you, but I will. My periods of lucidity

will grow less frequent, and random. I may be unable to explain myself." This next was the worst. "I'm assured that there will be personality changes. I might not speak to you in the way that I should. I might do bizarre things. With some people, there can even be a problem with aggression." There it was out.

"Here's what we've worked out," said Missy. "You're to let me know of each incident that happens. Adele will remain living here as long as possible. When the time comes that it's needed, we'll hire a nurse to be with her. That's what I need to rely on you for, to keep me apprised of how things are going so we can plan."

"We'll manage, I'm sure."

"No, that's not what I want," Adele said. "For now, I think we can manage with just us, but I will not have you putting up with something you shouldn't have to. That's why you are to tell Missy *everything* that happens. There's money to hire extra staff. If you feel that too much of your time is taken up with me, then we'll hire people to take over some of your duties." One side of her mouth quirked up. "Or Missy will."

"About Miss Annette," began Oliver.

"Annette knows nothing about my diagnosis and won't until Missy feels it's time. I'm hoping that will be a long time down the road. We know she won't be happy about it."

"Oh, course not. She'll worry about her grandmother."

Adele gave a half smile at Abigail. "Nice try, but we both know that Annette's chief concern will be about the money."

Well. There wasn't much to say about that.

Chapter Twenty-Seven

"Hey, Mel," Keira said over the phone. "Could we get together sometime soon?"

"As in a friendly get-together, or something professional."

"Professional. I need your autism advice."

"Is Daniel struggling? Things are going all right here at school, as far as I know."

Mel's office was, well, interesting. Cramped was one word. Plain brown curtains hid bookshelves from the eyes of visitors. Her bare, old desk held nothing but a closed laptop, the only adornment a sand art piece. When turned upside down, the colored sand flowed in a pleasing pattern to form a new sandscape. Even though there was no chalkboard in sight, somehow there was still the odor of old chalk dust.

"Is this an official meeting?" Mel asked. As the school district autism consultant, formal meetings meant more stringent note taking.

"Sort of, although not strictly education related. But it could affect Daniel's behavior here at school."

"What's going on?"

Keira puffed out some air. "It's a long story." She explained about Daniel's biological father showing up out of nowhere and demanding to meet his son. "From there it escalated. He not only wanted to meet Daniel, but to have a relationship with him."

"How's that going?"

"Not well. He's complained that I've raised a snooty kid because Daniel won't talk to him."

Both women shared a smile.

"I doubt he'd read any of the stuff on autism I suggested. Or at least if he did, none of it sank in. He's clueless."

"You've had five years to get used to the idea and to learn. It's not always easy for someone new to autism."

"Yeah, I get that. But on his first outing with Daniel, guess where he took him?"

Mel waited.

"Chuck E. Cheese."

Mel couldn't help it and laughter snorted out of her. "How did *that* go?"

"About as well as you'd imagine. Jake and I followed them to the restaurant just in case, and we walked in on Daniel in a full-blown meltdown." Her eyes narrowed. "Mason, that rat, just stood there, while his girlfriend screamed at him to do something, to shut his kid up. She was louder than Daniel."

"It might have gone all right if he'd been properly prepared, or taken it small steps at a time."

"I made a social story for Mason to use with him, but I don't think he looked at it even once."

"I'm sorry Daniel went through that. What would you like from me?"

"Mason is pushing forward with this, through a lawyer. The next thing he wants is to have Daniel stay with them for a weekend."

"Them?"

"Mason and his girlfriend." She caught Mel's look. "Yeah, *that* girlfriend, the same one who was in a screaming match with Daniel at Chuck E. Cheese."

"How much time have they spent together?"

"There's been four visits in my home, then that Chuck E. Cheese episode."

"And how do they get along?"

Keira shrugged. "Daniel plays alone on the floor while Mason sits there, thumbing through his phone." She thought about it. "To be fair, he tries to talk to Daniel, but when Daniel doesn't respond, he gives up. He has shown no signs of learning sign language and doesn't come with any kind of visuals."

"Does Daniel mind his presence?"

"He more or less ignores him. It's not like with Jake, where Daniel pulls him over to play with him, or snuggles. I'd say Daniel is more neutral toward Mason, neither liking nor disliking him."

"What would you like from me?"

"Obviously, Mason should not be in charge of Daniel, even for a day. He doesn't understand him, doesn't know what he needs. It would be a disaster if Daniel had to spend a weekend with them." She moved to the edge of her chair. "I need a report from you saying that it would be damaging for Mason to have him for a weekend."

Mel sat back and paused. "I don't know if I can do that."

"Why? Why not? It's obvious that this guy is clueless about autism."

"So are lots of people initially, but they learn."

"Daniel needs stability and routine. He hardly knows his father. It's just not going to work."

"You mentioned a lawyer. Is there a plan?"

"Unfortunately, yes. First Mason wanted a paternity test to prove he's Daniel's father."

"And?"

"Of course, the test was positive. If you saw the two together, you'd know - same reddish hair, same freckles, even the same walk. But he has no rights to Daniel. He walked out on me as soon as he learned I was pregnant, and we heard nothing from him until he began all this a month or so ago. Now he claims he wants a relationship with Daniel, to spend time with him."

"Do you have anything casting suspicions about this Mason being around a child? History of violence? Abuse?"

"No, nothing like that. My lawyer already checked."

"Let me get this right. Mason is the father, that's been proven."

Keira nodded.

"He disappears then shows up when Mason's seven and says he wants to be involved in his life."

"Yeah, that's right."

"Does he have an adequate place to live? Somewhere Daniel would be safe if he stayed overnight with him?"

"Yes. Mason lives with his girlfriend in a mansion that belongs to Annette's grandmother."

"I take it then that space, money for food, and adequate shelter aren't a problem."

"No."

"I'm no lawyer, but since he's the bio dad, it's my guess

that he has rights to see Daniel, even if this is a change of heart after seven years."

"That's what my lawyer said, and she thinks the courts will agree."

Mel waited.

"But he can't have Mason. He's *my* son. I've raised him; I've done everything on my own. He can't just waltz in here and say, sorry, I've changed my mind. I want my kid after all."

Mel said nothing.

"But he *can't* have him for a weekend. He just can't. He doesn't understand anything about autism, anything at all. How would he communicate with him? He could harm Daniel with his ignorance. What would he do if Daniel became overwhelmed? How would Daniel feel to be away from me for two entire nights? Autistic kids can't be shuttled back and forth between houses, between people. They need stability and predictability."

"True. Having things stable and predictable helps. But things can be stable even going between two homes or two parents."

Keira's voice rose. "How can you *say* that?"

"Because I've seen it repeatedly with students. Just because a child is autistic doesn't mean that the parents will remain together. In fact, there is a higher incident of marital breakdown when a child has special needs."

Keira glared at the woman she thought was a friend.

"I'm sorry. I'm not saying what you'd like to hear. But I'm telling you the truth. There are autistic kids who successfully spend time in the homes of two separate parents. He can get used to two sets of rules, two ways of doing things."

"Not happening with Daniel."

Mel paused. "I can only imagine how hard this is for you, especially coming out of the blue. It's not like Mason has been a presence in Daniel's life all along. Perhaps Daniel has the right to know his father. How could it hurt to have more people in his life who love him?" She pulled out a pen and pad of paper. "I could help you with some things, if you'd like."

"Like what?"

"We could draw up a calendar for Daniel, showing days when he'll be home with you and when he'll be with his dad. I'd recommend a social story for when he'll be at Mason's that includes a picture of the room where he'll sleep, toys he'll find there, the kitchen, bathroom, as well as pictures of the people he'll be with in the house." She thought for a moment. "And a schedule of how his day will look."

Keira stood. "That's not at all what I was thinking. Those things are fine for when he's with me, and they've helped a lot. But with Mason, I just want to shut this whole thing down. Daniel's been just fine with me all along. He has no need to get to know his birth father."

Chapter Twenty-Eight

Keira, Mason and their lawyers sat in front of Judge Bursey in his chambers. National and state flags stood in the corners. The prevalence of heavy wood added to the officious atmosphere.

"Thank you all for being here. For now, I'd like to hear directly from the parents." He checked his notes. "I understand that this is a custody dispute."

"No!" burst from Keira. "This is about visitation, not custody."

Judge Bursey scanned the documents again, then raised his eyes. "Mr. Cooper, is custody your intention?"

Mason glanced at Keira out of the corner of his eye and pulled his legs in under his chair. "Yes, Your Honor."

"What!" Keira was on her feet.

"Sit down, Ms. Foster." He looked at Julie Franco, Keira's lawyer. "I take it you two haven't discussed this?"

"No, Your Honor. The papers requesting custody just arrived at my office this morning, even though they are dated a week and a half ago." She glared at her opposing counsel.

Keira whirled. "Custody? He's *my* son. I've raised him." She turned on Mason. "You! You abandoned us, you ran out, saying you wanted no part of a kid. Then, over seven years later, you suddenly appear, saying you want to see your son. To have custody?"

"Is that true, Mr. Cooper?" Judge Bursey asked.

"Sorta. Yeah, I didn't want a kid back then. Hell, I was just a kid myself." Mason squirmed. "But I'm older now, more mature and know my duty. I'm in a relationship and we want a family, want my son."

"It's a child we're talking about, *my* child. Not a car or even a cat. You can't just suddenly decide you want him after all this time."

"Ms. Foster, please sit down." Judge Bursey looked between Keira and Mason. "As I understand it, there has been no contact between the child and Mr. Cooper since the birth?"

"Since before the birth," Keira corrected. "He ran out as soon as he heard I was pregnant."

"But you've been paying child support all along." This was directed at Mason as more a statement requiring confirmation, rather than a question.

Keira snorted.

"Ah, no, Your Honor," admitted Mason. "But I'm in a position now to pay child support."

"Hmph." Judge Bursey straightened the papers in front of him. "Let's back up to when contact began." His gaze was just for Mason now. "Have you met the child?"

Mason nodded.

"How many times have you seen him."

"Four times."

"And where was that?"

"At Keira's house, then once we tried to take him to a restaurant."

"Tried, Mr. Cooper?"

"Yeah. We got there and were waiting for a table, but the kid freaked out."

"Why would that be?"

Keira interrupted. "They tried to take him to a Chuck E. Cheese. Daniel is autistic and the noise and atmosphere there was too much for him, and he got overwhelmed."

"I see." The Judge thought. "Could this have been handled differently, Ms. Foster?"

"Well, yes. They could have gone to a different restaurant. They could have prepared Daniel for what he'd encounter there. They could have taken him when it wouldn't be crowded."

"Did they ask your opinion on this?"

"No!"

"Mr. Cooper, what do you have to say about this?"

"Chuck E. Cheese is known to be a favorite with kids. Daniel's a kid, so we thought we'd give him a treat. It certainly wouldn't be *our* choice for a date night, be we tried to do something special for my son."

Judge Bursey regarded Mason for a bit. "Well, you're not the first parent to make an error in judgement and you won't be the last." He moved his gaze to take in the lawyers near the back of the room. "What is the plan?"

"Your Honor," began Mason's lawyer. "We're willing to take this slowly, for the sake of the child. The next step is for Daniel to spend a weekend with his dad."

Judge Bursey turned his look to Mason. "Do you have adequate accommodations for a child?"

"Yes, sir, more than adequate. My girlfriend and I live

with her grandmother in an estate. We have our own wing that has three bedrooms, each with its own bathroom. Our suite has a living room, plus another area we've turned into a playroom. In the rest of the house there's a theatre, a games room. A cook and other household staff see to the meals and cleaning. There're acres of lawn to play on, plus a swimming pool."

"Who would supervise the child while he was with you?"

"Me. I'll be there the whole time, along with my girl-friend, Annette Henry. Her grandmother might be around sometimes, too, but she's old, so won't be on the floor playing with him."

"How old is old?"

"Not sure exactly, but she's in her early 70s."

The judge's brows lowered, but he ignored that remark. "When is this visit planned?"

Mason's lawyer spoke up. "No date has been agreed on yet, but we were hoping for this coming weekend. Keep the momentum going, you know."

"No!" Keira stood again.

Judge Bursey joined her on his feet. "This weekend it is." To Keira he said, "I presume the child is in school?"

She nodded.

Bursey addressed this to the lawyers. "Make arrangements for the visit to begin sometime the afternoon of Friday, the 15th after school, to be returned to his mother the afternoon of the 17th." He stopped in his departure and questioned Mason. "I almost forgot to ask. Does the child know you're his father?"

Mason shook his head, looking at Keira for confirmation.

"When is he going to know?"

Keira didn't remember getting from the judge's office to her car. She sat there trembling, her fists wrapped around the steering wheel, trying to ground herself. It was all slipping away, this life she'd built so carefully for herself and her son. Everything she'd done to create their security, their safe haven, the protective bubble where Daniel could flourish, never at risk of facing the heartache of rejection Keira went through.

Her phone vibrated in her pocket, sound having been turned off while with the Judge. Judge. That word meant deciding about someone or something, especially after reflecting. How could the Judge have decided in favor of Mason? Could he not see just what a rat fink the man was? Deserting his pregnant girlfriend. Running out on them. Leaving her destitute and never looking back. Then springing up out of nowhere, making claims on his son. His son. Huh. Like giving sperm made the man a father with rights.

The cell phone took up its annoying hum again. Keira reached into her pocket to look at the number. It had better not be the rat fink himself, calling to gloat.

Jake. It was Jake. The tightness in Keira's shoulders loosened at least somewhat. She let out a breath and put her head against the high-backed seat. "Hello."

"Hey, how'd it go?" It irked him no end that he couldn't have been there with her.

"Oh, Jake." Now the tears came. Not for herself, but for Daniel.

"What is it?" His worst fear was that somehow the Court might award custody to Mason Cooper. No matter how much money Jake and Keira piled together, they'd never be able to match the amount Mason's girlfriend had at her disposal. Too often, money talked.

She related what had gone on in the Chambers - that the goal was shared custody, that they wanted her son for the weekend.

"*This* weekend?" He blew out a breath. "Okay, we've got this. What do we need to do to prepare Daniel?"

Keira looked at the phone. He was right. As devastating as this was to Keira and what she believed right, Daniel was the priority. If protecting and helping him meant prepping him for time with his birth father, then prep they would.

"Thanks."

"For what?"

"For reminding me of what we need to do. I was too busy wallowing."

We. She'd said 'we'. Progress. At least she hadn't mentioned taking Daniel and running.

Maybe he could deepen that 'we'. After all, wouldn't a committed significant other suggest more of a stable environment than a single mom could provide? This was not the time to raise such ideas, though.

Chapter Twenty-Nine

Adele

It was one of those days, the bad ones. The disquiet started as soon as Adele opened her eyes.

She'd dreamt her wedding ring had fallen into her bowl of French onion soup. The soup was a clear broth, or nearly clear, but every time she dipped her spoon into the bowl to retrieve it, her eyes could not penetrate the murk of the swirling shades of brown to scoop out that ring. That precious ring, the one Hubert had given her when he asked her to marry him. It was at an outdoor bistro in Paris. When she'd leapt from her chair to throw her arms around Hubert, the whole cafe erupted in applause. That had begun their fairy tale life together, ending only upon Hubert's death.

That was a dark time, meshed in walls of grief. The light of her life, gone. The linchpin of her everything. That was Hubert. Calm, capable, so in charge.

He never complained about the responsibility of thousands of employees, how the livelihood of so many rested on his shoulders, on him making the right decisions. He just did it, soldiering on, as had his father before him, and his grandfather before that.

He'd talked about an old saying - the first generation creates the wealth, the second generation builds on it, the third generation squanders it. Hubert was that third generation. But the adage was untrue. Hubert had doubled the family's holdings since he became of age. The growth was slow at first, until his father retired, handing the reins to Hubert.

It wasn't exactly the money that drove Hubert, but the challenge. They already had all they could ever need, but there was this obligation to build, to expand on the legacy, the need to better the lives of those who helped them along the way. Employees, *all* employees received shares. When the company prospered, they prospered. When the company suffered downturns, well, they had cushions built in to absorb that. Adele worked with the HR departments to develop the employee day care programs and health plans, the best in the state.

Life was good and then got better with the birth of their son Jason. A joy. Did they pamper him? Maybe a little, especially Adele, who came from more humble means. To shower Jason with the best was a pleasure.

Perhaps less so in his teen years. When had he turned from grateful to needy, to entitled? He'd grow out of it, she'd assured Hubert. It was just a growing-up phase.

When it came time for college, donations helped pave the way to admissions that grades alone wouldn't allow. But he'd settle down once he found his niche, hopefully one related to business to help build the family empire.

That's where Jason met Rachel, a sweetheart, if a little

vacuous. Rachel quit college in her second year to 'find herself'. Easy to spend time in that search when she lived with Jason, supported by the Henry family trust fund.

Hubert scowled as he checked the bank statements of Jason's trust, noting the rapid decline in capital. There was enough there to support a family for life, but at this rate, it was uncertain if it would see Jason through his degree. When confronted, Jason solved the problem - he quit school. What did he need a degree for? There were jobs just waiting for him. That is, if he wanted them.

Disgruntled with the type of accommodation his now scaled-back funds allowed, Jason and Rachel moved in with Adele and Hubert. They saw little of each other with the kids hanging out in their own wing of the mansion and demanding that meals be served in their private dining room at hours that suited their needs. Reminders that's not how we treat staff went unheeded, especially during the flurry of preparations for their fairy tale wedding.

But all was forgiven and forgotten when Jason and Rachel presented them with their grandchild, the absolutely perfect baby, Annette.

Motherhood didn't come naturally to all women. Some needed to grow into the role, Adele and Hubert assured themselves. In the meantime, they had the money to provide a nanny, plus there were the doting grandparents lavishing attention on the little princess.

They never discussed that nagging worry that Adele did far more for the child than did either of the parents, that is, until that dark day word came about the skiing accident.

Enjoying their play, Jason and Rachel often indulged in helicopter skiing, the thrill of starting down a pristine mountainside, conquering the slope. But this one time, the mountain held the cards, sending tons of packed snow careening down upon the two. Eventually, Jason's body was found, but Rachel's not until the following spring.

Improvident to the end, Jason died intestate, despite Hubert's urging, especially when Jason had a wife and child. While the weight of childcare now fell to Adele, the legal and financial matters consumed Hubert.

With their loss heavy on their hearts, not surprisingly, the grandparents did all they could to make it up to Annette. Whether nature or nurture, Annette took after her father's ways, with enjoying money being her primary pastime, rather than increasing their family's fortune. Why bother?

Adele rolled over, dangling her legs off the side of the bed, one foot idly searching for its slipper. Not where it should be.

The room felt hazy, the furniture indistinct. But how could that be? Turning her head, a sharp edge on a dresser took shape. Looking at it head on, though, it seemed in shadows, the lines wavy and undulating.

Or maybe it was her undulating.

Pressure on her bladder propelled her forward. A recessed corner of her brain reassured her that the ensuite bathroom was there, just a few feet through a doorway. But in which direction?

Why were old memories so clear? Easy to conjure up the pain of learning that their only child was dead. The shame of giving bonuses to household staff mistreated by Jason and Rachel. Lifting a crying Annette out of her crib while the child's parents slept in the next room. Finding her way to the opposite end of the house in the dark was a snap, but why could she not find the way to her own bathroom now?

Erect, if swaying, she willed her feet to move in the right

direction. They dragged. Since when did she shuffle like an old lady?

Her toe snagged on the trailing edge of her dressing gown. How could something so satiny bring her down? Righting herself was tricky, then impossible. She felt her bladder let loose from the exertion. Her hands flailed. She called out for Hubert just before her left temple cracked on the corner of a bureau. Hubert's bureau. She'd remind him to move it when he got home from work tonight. Then, the haze was replaced with nothing.

"Missus, missus, wake up!"

Adele groaned.

"Missus, it's me, Abigail. Are you all right? Please speak to me."

Abigail. Why was she disturbing her? All she wanted to do was sleep. So tired.

"Oliver, call the ambulance." Only when Abigail lifted her employer's head to slide a pillow under it did she notice the blood. Silvery grey hairs were matted with it, drying in a coagulated mass on the plush burgundy carpeting.

Missy met them at the hospital. A concussion, yes, but was there even more damage?

It took until the next day for Adele to truly rouse. White padded gauze bandages hid the extent of the damage to the side of her head, although the purplish-black bruising extended down past her cheek bone. The old Adele was back, joking that she'd tried to knock some sense into her temporal lobe, the one giving her so much grief these days. The doctor said her aim was slightly off and she'd caught more of her frontal lobe than the temporal. But both needed a shaking up, in Adele's opinion.

New plans, with the help of a neuropsychologist. They talked about strategies, not cures, patches, rather than fixes.

Labels were put everywhere in that section of the house. A sign on the door to the bathroom. Each dresser drawer labeled. A sign on the suite's door pointed the way downstairs.

Then the stairs themselves. Even though she'd trod them for two-thirds of her life, now they posed a threat. After considering and rejecting a variety of lifts, construction began on an elevator to run from the bottom floor to the top.

"Why do we need all these strangers in the house?" Annette was not a happy camper. "I like my privacy, and I need my sleep." When no one paid her complaints heed, Annette fled. St. Tropez was lovely this time of year.

The workers Missy hired began work at seven each morning, and were told to only take orders from Missy, Abigail, or Oliver. The sawing, banging, grating, the rapid-fire chug chug of the cordless drills shattered the normally silent mansion from sunrise to sundown. Construction took a little longer than needed to be given the building's heritage value and the necessity of making this new addition blend into the decor. Money could do that, though.

Chapter Thirty

"Aren't you coming back?" Mason winced. Was that a whine in his voice? He tried again. "This is the weekend Daniel's coming. Don't you want to be here?"

Annette yawned. It was mid-morning in St. Tropez. She'd been having such a lovely sleep when Mason's call woke her.

"I have too much going on here to get back that soon." She smiled at the opulent room, furnished much more to her liking than the way her grandmother kept her old mausoleum of a house. Heavy, with all that wood. No, Annette much preferred the pale colors and gilded accents of the French provincial decor.

"But this is important." How could he do it on his own?

"Of course it is, darling. That's why you're on it. I have faith in you."

"But…"

She needed to cut this short. "The little guy will be much more comfortable with just you. He knows you well now. Too many new people would confuse him." She could still probably get in another hour or two of sleep to prepare her for the activities that would last well into the night. "But I want to hear all about it afterwards." She blew kisses into the phone, then hung up.

While Mel had been a disappointment, Anna would not be. Never. Anna was on her side, a friend. Plus, as a social worker specializing in child welfare, she'd know.

They met for lunch near to the courthouse where Anna worked.

Small talk lasted only a few minutes before Keira started. She filled Anna in on what had happened over the last few weeks since Mason first contacted her, then exploded into their lives.

Anna nodded. "I can see Judge Bursey supporting visits with this Mason. We've come full circle. Decades ago, it was the fathers who had all the power. Then that shifted into the mothers' court, but now it's recognized that fathers have rights too, even absentee fathers."

"It's not right, you know."

Anna gave a half-smile. "How does Daniel feel about having his father in his life?"

Keira was silent.

"Ah, he doesn't know?"

"I thought you said they've met several times."

"They have."

"How'd you introduce Mason?"

"As a friend. I hated to call him that, but couldn't think of any other word to use. Sewer rat, although appropriate, didn't seem quite the label to use." She shrugged. "Other than that, we just use the name Mason."

"Doesn't Daniel wonder why he's going with this man?"

"For that Chuck E. Cheese fiasco, we just told him he was going out for something to eat. He didn't want to go, but Jake strapped him into their car and told him it was all right. It wasn't though."

"Not the best choice for his first outing with his father. Did you try to dissuade Mason?"

"Of course I did! But he wouldn't listen. And maybe there was an off chance that it could work. I can't always predict what will be too much for Daniel."

"Now you're wondering if you should leave things as they are, with Daniel believing the man is just a friend, or if you should tell him Mason is his father."

"Yeah." Keira slumped into her chair. "Telling him makes it seem, so, I don't know, permanent or something."

"Isn't it permanent?"

"With Mason's history, I doubt it. If he could bolt on us once, what's stopping him from doing it again?"

"Age, maturity, stability, a sense of responsibility, genuine caring for a child."

Only one corner of Keira's mouth turned up. "That's you, Anna. Always with the positive spin. I don't know how you still see the good in people after everything you've been through."

"I don't, not everyone, that is. But this Mason is sort of an unknown quantity, even if you knew him seven years ago. There must have been something decent about the guy for you to be attracted to him initially."

"I was a stupid kid."

"Somehow, I don't think that's true."

"Well one with poor judgement."

"People in their early 20s aren't known for their wisdom."

"What do you think? Should I tell Daniel?"

"From what I've seen of the two of you, you have a good relationship, an honest one. How would Daniel feel later on if he learned that you'd kept something as important as this from him? And what if Mason or his girlfriend let it slip that Daniel is his son? Would Daniel feel betrayed that you'd kept that a secret?"

"Whoa. Stop with the trying to make me feel good stuff."

Anna laughed. "You asked."

"Yeah, I did, because I trust your opinion. I'll talk to Jake tonight. I'd like him to be there in case I choke."

"Daniel, come sit with us a moment, please. I need to tell you something." Keira moved over to make room on the couch for Daniel to squeeze between her and Jake.

When he'd tucked himself in to his satisfaction, she started. "You know the man, Mason, who's come to visit you?"

Daniel nodded and waited.

"I, he…" The words just wouldn't come. Her eyes asked Jake for help.

Jake got it. "You know how when Brendan and Elizabeth got married, that meant that Timothy got a new dad?" They'd all attended the quiet wedding last summer.

Daniel waited some more, glancing back at his puzzle on the floor.

This wasn't that easy. How to explain something as complicated as parenthood without getting into the birds and the bees?

Jake cleared his throat. "Brendan is his dad now, but before that Timothy had another dad, the dad who was there when he was born."

"Two." Daniel got it.

"Yeah, he has two dads." Jake skipped the part about the original father being in jail now for kidnapping Elizabeth and her son and trying to kill his son's mother. There was only so much reality you should thrust upon a seven-year-old.

Keira felt able to continue now. "You see, Mason was your father at the time you were born."

Daniel's eyes widened.

Unsure how to explain, Keira rushed on. "He wasn't there, so he didn't know you. He only came by recently and said he wanted to get to know you. He's your dad."

At the word father, Daniel's head turned to Jake. "Dad?"

Jake swallowed hard. Dad. What he wouldn't give to have the right for this boy to call him that. One day, but for now... He gathered the boy to him. "We're friends, you and me, the best of buddies, but I'm not your father. I only met you three years ago. Your father knew you before you were even born." This sucked.

Leaning back in Jake's arms, Daniel looked from the man who held him securely to his mom and back again. Then he buried his face in Jake's chest.

Jake looked at Keira, a sheen of tears in both their eyes. He pulled Daniel in closer. "It's fine, bud. We're tight, you and me, and I'm not going anywhere." His gaze lifted to Keira's again.

She nodded.

While the emotion remained with the two adults, Daniel soon returned to his puzzles on the floor, as if his little world had not just rocked. Maybe for him it hadn't.

At least that's what Keira and Jake hoped as they sipped their coffee in the kitchen.

"It could have gone worse," said Keira.

"Not sure what I expected, but he seemed okay with it."

"It might take him time to process the news."

"It's tough when he can't voice the questions or thoughts that must be running around in his head."

The term dad was just a word, an abstract identity Daniel had never experienced. At least before Jake entered their lives.

Who knew how much a kid took in about relationships? His friends certainly had variation in their households. In fact, the only family unit he'd encountered with the typical mother, father and children was that of Natalie, a teen who babysat Daniel and his friends a few times. Daniel hadn't liked Natalie and made that clear. His instincts were spot on, they later found out.

His friend, Amy, lived with just her mother. Until recently, Timothy had lived only with his mother, prior to her marriage to Brendan. Bonnie lived with her adopted parents and brother. Likely, for Daniel, such things just were without the complications of how these relationships came to be.

But none of these kids shuttled back and forth between two households. For an autistic kid craving stability, how would *that* work?

Then it was time for bath and bed for Daniel. He chose Jake to read him his bedtime story.

Settled back in the living room, they sipped the hot toddies Keira had made.

"What's the worst that could happen?" Keira needed to talk this out.

"Maybe that Mason wants to share custody of Daniel." He felt Keira tense beneath his arm.

"I've thought about that. Can't see how a Court would

ever give him custody when he made himself scarce all these years and took no responsibility for his son, no attempts to even see how he was."

"Makes sense." But in his experience in law enforcement, the logical outcome was not always the one that stuck.

"Besides, Mason is a here-today-gone-tomorrow kind of guy. No sticking power. Parenting isn't easy, especially when the child has different needs. I think he'll get tired of putting in the effort."

"True. And his girlfriend didn't seem like the nurturing type, either. I'm sure they'll tire of the novelty of Mason being a father or have kids of their own."

"Yeah. It'll all be fine."

Chapter Thirty-One

Daniel lifted the backpack onto his shoulders. Mom had put his clothes and toothbrush in there but left room for toys. Heavy. That's okay. Weight was comforting, especially when facing new stuff.

He removed the lid from the 18-gallon Rubbermaid plastic container. All around his bedroom, toys lay scattered as he'd searched through, finding the right stuff. This was tough. Mom said to pack what he might want to play with over the weekend. How did you do that? Who knew what you'd feel like doing? She'd given him a five-gallon tote to fill, but it held hardly anything at all. Good thing there was this bigger one in the garage. It only held old clothes that didn't matter. They were fine on the floor until he put them back later.

Dad. They said Mason was his dad. What was he supposed to call him? Timothy used to call his Brendan Brendan, but now called him dad. But that didn't feel right. If anyone was dad, it was Jake, not Mason. Better not to call him anything.

The doorbell rang. Already? No, he needed more time. What if he left something important behind? Really wanted to play with something he hadn't packed with it? Would they let him come home to get it?

It was rising up, that big pocket of air in his gut, threatening to block off his air. No room to suck in oxygen. He needed oxygen for his brain to function. Breathe, Daniel, breathe, mom always said. Eyes closed, picturing a square. A big breath in along the top of the square, hold it in along the right side of the square, let it out along the bottom leg, rest going up the left side. Again. And again.

It worked; it almost always did. Slowly, the panic receded, then Jake was there.

"Hey, bud, ready to go?"

Jake's voice sounded funny, that too cheerful way grownups got when they were trying to suck you in.

Jake took his hand and started toward the door. "Mason's here for you."

Daniel resisted the tug on his hand and nudged the large tote with his foot.

"What? No. You don't mean that goes with you?"

Yes, Jake got it.

"Okay. I don't know what your mom's going to say, but I'll carry it downstairs."

Mom and the man, Mason, stood in the entryway, watching Jake lug the Rubbermaid container.

Mom frowned. "Where'd you get that, Daniel? That's not the tote I gave you."

Mom and Jake shared a look. "Guess a guy never knows what he might need, so he better be prepared, right bud?" Jake put an arm around his shoulder, giving a squeeze.

"I guess it's fine." Mom's voice didn't match her words. "Okay with you, Mason?"

"Sure. He'll have his own bedroom, plus a playroom to spread out in. Lots of room for his stuff and the new toys I bought for him."

New toys? Interesting. Maybe this wouldn't be so bad.

"I'll carry this out to the car." Jake left.

Left. That didn't feel so good. And Mom looked funny. The corners of her mouth went up, but her eyes looked what? Tired? Sad? Scared? It was so hard to tell. Maybe something was wrong with her. Maybe this wasn't such a good idea.

"Let's go, then." Mason had that fake, happy tone in his voice.

This wasn't right. He should just stay here with Mom and Jake. "No."

"The first time the kid speaks to me, and it's the word 'no,'" Mason muttered.

Jake was back. "Ready to go?"

No. That bubble made its way up again, getting higher, pushing up into his lungs so there was no room to get in air. Rising onto toes helped, as did the squeal.

"What's wrong with the kid? Why's he making that noise?"

Mason looked scared, too. This was all wrong. He needed to stay here with Mommy.

Jake knelt down. "It's okay, bud. You'll be all right. Take some big breaths in. Do it with me, now."

Helped. Helped a bit. The last time they made me go with Mason, it was bad. Chuck E. Cheese was supposed to be a fun kids' place, but it wasn't. Not one bit.

"Why don't we go with you?" Mom suggested to Mason. "We'll follow you and help Daniel get used to this new place."

"Will he stop that squealing?"

Mom gave the man a bad look.

"All right, but he rides with me. He's gotta get used to me and we can't pamper the kid all the time." Grabbing the backpack, Mason left the house. The backpack with most important stuff.

This time, the Maserati didn't smell awful, without that woman in it. It just smelled right. Ah, the seats with the smoothest of leathers. Soft and just slightly warm. Smooth and yielding, the kind of surface inviting fingers to brush it over and over. Ah, calming. Maybe this would be okay.

They waited behind the car containing Mason and Daniel while Mason opened the gates at the entrance to the estate. Towering, black wrought iron doors parted in the middle, folding back to allow them in. Behind Jake's truck, the gates closed with barely a clank.

Following Mason, they pulled up to the massive front door, surveying the sprawling lawns. "Wow, you could fit an entire football field in here without even damaging any of the flower beds."

"He said the estate sits on five acres." Keira checked out the area with a mother's eye. From the vast open areas with shimmering grass, trees dotted sections, and a hedge perimeter inside of fencing similar to the gate they'd just come through. "A kid could get lost here."

Daniel climbed out of the Maserati, clutching his backpack. Mason's hand on his shoulder urged him forward. No! Where were Mommy and Jake?

There. Each of them took a position by his side. Jake's hand gently urged him forward.

One half of the front door opened, although it was a door unlike anything typical. Like the front gate, it was dome-shaped and split down the middle. A smiling woman waited. She crouched down on one knee. "Daniel, welcome. We are so looking forward to your visit. I'm Abigail." She held out her hand.

A look from Mom reminded him of his manners, and he shook her hand. Hands could be yucky or all right. This one wasn't damp or sticky, but warm and sort of smooth. The lady gave a quick squeeze, then let go. Thank goodness.

"Abigail, this is Daniel, as you've guessed." Then, pointed to Keira, "And this is Daniel's mother, Keira, and her boyfriend, Jake." The woman shook their hands.

"Come in, come in. Mrs. Henry is so eager to meet you." The lady stood to the side, then shut the door behind them.

Mason led the way across the marble foyer. Their footsteps echoed. It would be better if everyone took off their shoes, easier on the ears, but no one did. At least his hands were free to cover his ears.

An old lady sat in a velvety, golden chair. Her hair was all white, but soft-looking. She had a nice smile, not the fake kind.

"Adele, I'd like you to meet my son, Daniel."

"Come here, little boy. I have my reading glasses on and can't see all the way across the room."

Little boy. There was only one little boy in the room, so… She didn't look scary.

Mason pushed on his shoulder just enough to make him dig in his heels.

Then Mom took his hand and walked with him to the old lady. Except something was wrong with her glasses; there was only the bottom half and empty space where the rest of the glass was supposed to be.

"Hi. I'm Keira Foster and this is *my* son, Daniel."

The old lady held out a hand for Mom to shake. "You've raised a lovely boy."

"We think he's pretty special," said Jake. "Hi, I'm Jake, the guy who's been hanging around these two for the last few years." He put one arm around Mom.

"I bet you'd love to see your bedroom," the old lady said.

"Come right this way," said Abigail. "We think you'll like your room. The bed looks like Maserati." She took his hand and started up the staircase, the bigger one ever. And it wasn't straight but curved. Nice, pleasing lines. The thick carpet muffled their steps, much nicer than the hard marble in the hallway.

Abigail continued. "And wait 'til you see the playroom. We bought new ones but have shelves for all your favorite toys."

Toys. Wait. His feet froze to the stair tread. Toys. Were they lost? That bubble started to make its way up. Jake Had had carried it out of the house. Where was Jake?

"What's wrong, Daniel? Don't you want to see the new toys?" Mom was right there, but it was Jake who got it.

"Be right back, bud. I'll bring in your toys."

Phew.

It was nice. A mattress tucked inside a bright yellow car bed. A desk. An easel with paints and colored chalk. A closet with shelves at his level, just like at home.

"Come see the playroom next door." Abigail again.

Wow. A climbing fort with a castle on top. More Lego than even the store contained. A wooden rack full of jigsaw puzzles, and empty open shelves.

Jake set the Rubbermaid tote beside the shelves. "Shall I help you put these on the shelves?" That seemed rather permanent, like they might be there to stay. No, they were okay in the tote. He shook his head.

"There's lots to play with here, son. Give me a hug, and Jake and I'll go, but see you later." Mom's voice sounded funny.

Abigail got a puzzle from the rack and set it on the child-sized table. "Would you help me do this?"

Mason stood back and Mom and Jake left the room, then stood in the doorway watching.

"That was even harder than I thought," Keira told Jake from the familiar confines of his truck.

"The old lady seemed okay."

"Yeah." She was silent for the next few miles. "Pretty hard to compete with all they have to offer him."

"Keira, come on. You have exactly what Daniel needs - you. The rest is just stuff."

"Hmmm."

Chapter Thirty-Two

Lunch was a silent affair for Jake and Keira. She'd tried to urge him to go home, go do something, because she was miserable company, but no way he was leaving her alone.

"Think of this as one of those times Daniel is away on a play date with Timothy or Amy. You know where he is. He's safe and having fun. Then he'll be home."

He caught Keira looking at him with disbelief.

One thing about this woman, she was the most grounded he'd ever met. Solidly based in reality. She couldn't even fool her own mind into believing this was just another fun outing for her son. Nope, not his Keira.

Jake poured their tomato soup into bowls. It was from a can, but he'd snipped a couple of basil leaves off the herbs growing on the windowsill and plunked them in the middle of each bowl. Surely that counted for something. Grabbing two plates from the cupboard, he flipped the nicely browned grilled cheese sandwiches onto plates and brought their meal to the table where Keira sat fiddling with the edges of the woven placemat.

She looked up with a smile of thanks.

Out of habit, Jake skirted around the chair Daniel usually used to take his seat across from Keira.

Keira stared at the empty third chair. "You know, my parents always had empty chairs at the table."

Almost never had Keira spoken to him about her parents, apart from the initial explanation of why and when they'd disowned her.

"You want me to push Daniel's chair out of the way?"

"No!"

Okay, then.

Keira needed to talk. "We always had two extra places at the table. There was a setting for dad, mom, and me, then one for each of my sisters."

This was the first Jake had heard of siblings. He'd thought she was an only child.

"One was a chair with a booster seat tied to it. The cutlery was a plastic spoon and fork, the plate more of a round dish with sides. It was where my sister used to sit." As if talking to herself, Keira continued. "She died when she was two-and-a-half. I was four. I still remember her a bit, I think. Or maybe I just remember her plate because I saw it every day I lived at home."

"What happened to her?"

"Meningitis. Bacterial. We never knew how she contracted it, but the inflammation spread quickly. She was sick less than a week, then gone. Just gone."

"Oh, god, Keira. I'm so sorry."

"I'm not sure I understood what was going on. She was there and then she wasn't. They didn't let me go to the hospital to see her. Maybe they were afraid that I'd catch it, or maybe they were trying to protect me. I had to go stay at a neighbor's house. I could see my home from my front window, but they wouldn't let me go home. Not even when my parents' car was in the driveway. I didn't see my mother or father for a week."

Jake didn't think she even felt the tear trailing down one cheek.

"Then they were home and things were back to normal, except that my sister's chair was empty. Jackie, her name was. She wasn't there, but her dish and fork and spoon were, each and every time we sat down for a meal. From then until I left to go to college."

What was with those people? What a strange mausoleum for a dead child.

"Then Mom got pregnant. I didn't know what it meant, just thought she got fat. Dad spent hours in the garage at night. He had a workshop there. Then one night, just before supper, he brought in this highchair. Mom oohed and ahed over it. That's what he'd been building. It was all shiny wood with a seat and a belt and a tray they pulled up to the table. They were all excited about it, but I didn't get it. Yeah, it was shiny, and maybe sort of pretty. They explained that soon there would be a baby, and when the baby was old enough, she'd join us at the table for meals."

Jake noted the furniture Keira chose for her own kitchen. Everything was wooden - the table, chairs, the stools pulled up to the bar area, the butcher block counters.

"Then when Mom got really fat, I had to go stay at the neighbor's again, but this time just for a night. Then my parents came home, but there was no baby. She was stillborn."

Jake squeezed her hand.

"Her name was Mila. They'd had the name all picked out and etched it into the highchair. They didn't have a dish or cutlery ready for her, though. But by the time she would have been six months old, a set suddenly appeared and stayed on her highchair for every meal."

"Good lord, Keira."

"Yeah, I know. Kinda weird, isn't it? But back then, it seemed normal."

Normal? Not by a long shot.

"There's more. My parents wanted to keep the memories of my sisters alive. Every year, we'd celebrate their birthdays." She raised her eyes to him. "Yeah, I get now how strange that was, but it just was the way things were then. And what kid is going to complain about getting to eat birthday cake three times a year?"

"Why? Why the hell did they do that? Put you through that and themselves?"

"They said that family was sacred. We should never forget the family members we have or had."

"But they threw you out."

"I know."

"Want to go out for dinner?" They needed to do something to get out of this funk, Jake thought.

"No, thanks. I should be here in case Daniel needs me."

"Keira, you have your phone with you. I have mine. They'd call these numbers if you're needed."

"Yeah." That was true. Somehow, she felt she needed to remain within these four walls, the walls she lived in with Daniel.

"Then let's go pick up something and bring it back here to eat." He needed to get her out of the house, if only into the fresh air for a brief time, something to break the morose mood. "He's gone overnight, not permanently."

"I know. It's just… a bad feeling, I guess."

"Come on." Jake stood with Keira's jacket held up, ready for her to put her arms in.

Once in the car, the atmosphere felt at least somewhat better.

"What kind of food do you feel like?"

"I'm not really hungry. Maybe just something I can pick at. A pizza? No, I know. Let's get a charcuterie." She and Daniel had enjoyed their last one together.

Jake switched lanes and headed toward the mall that housed the Char Cut Roastery, Keira's favorite spot for charcuterie takeout.

They stood pursuing the board, debating their choices. "Sure, Daniel can pack it away sometimes, but you may have noticed that I eat more than him. What the two of you got last time won't cut it when I'm eating. Get something more."

Keira dutifully turned back to the menu board, but not before patting Jake's almost non-existent belly. "If you're sure you need more…" That was something the old Keira would do. Maybe they'd make it through this night.

A voice behind them spoke. "Keira?"

Keira froze.

Jake glanced at the tense woman at his side. During the drive here she'd relaxed, but now was more rigid than ever. He turned to see who had spoken.

An older woman stood behind them. Timid was the word that came to mind, not the kind to butt in on a stranger's conversation. Yet she had spoken Keira's name. Had she heard him use it? "Excuse us." He tugged on Keira's arm to move her to the side. Maybe the older woman wanted to check out the menu and had trouble peering over their shoulders. She was on the short side.

"Keira." The woman spoke again, but this time it wasn't a question.

Keira half-turned, almost as if her feet weren't obeying her brain.

"Where's your little boy?"

Who was this woman? How did she know Keira had a son? He took a half step in front of Keira.

"He's with his father."

What? Why had Keira answered this woman? What business was it of hers where Daniel was?

The woman spoke to Jake this time. "You're not the father?"

Okay, what was happening. "Keira, what's going on?"

Keira put her hand through his arm. "Jake, this is my... mother."

Mother? While he knew she had had one, Jake never believed he'd meet the woman who'd thrown Keira out of the house when she got pregnant. Well, he had a few things he wanted to say to a mother who could do that to a daughter, especially a daughter as wonderful as Keira. He opened his mouth, but no words came out. He saw the pleading in the older woman's eyes, the sorrow, the apology, the fear of rejection. His heart hardened again. Rejection. She should feel what it was like. He could only imagine how terrified and alone Keira had felt after Mason's desertion, then her own parents disowning her in her time of need.

"Mom, this is Jake Dean." There was a waver in her voice, one Jake had not heard before.

Looking between the two women now, the resemblance was unmistakable. Jake didn't know how he had missed it before. But where Keira's shoulders had grown firmer, more confident over the years, this woman's shoulders bowed with the look of a dog who didn't know if he'd be thrown scraps or booted in the side.

"When I saw you the other time, I wanted to come over, but didn't dare. Your boy's - he's beautiful, and so big."

"He's seven. It's been over seven years."

"I know. I know exactly how long it's been. I relive that day over and over in my mind, wishing we could take it back, that we had another chance." Her eyes filled with tears. "Your dad and me both."

"Right."

The hard Keira was back, the feisty woman Jake had first met, the one willing to take on the world for herself and her son. The one she'd needed to be to survive. He put an arm around her shoulders, drawing her closer, relieved when she let him.

The older woman spoke despite the rivulets of tears coursing down her cheeks. "We looked for you. The next day. We looked everywhere, but you were gone, just gone. The college wouldn't give us any information about you, even if you were still enrolled. Confidentiality, they said. You had taken us off your contact list as next of kin with them, so they would not tell us anything. We had your young man's phone number, but he never answered any of our calls. We just lost you."

"That was what you wanted, you said."

"We didn't mean it. Your father didn't mean the things he said and I, I was too shocked to think of any words. This was not what we hoped for our little girl."

"Yeah, I got that." Jake had never heard Keira speak with such bitterness.

"But you were our child, our only child, and we loved you. Still do."

"Riiight. Somehow, 'Get out and never come back' doesn't speak of unswerving love."

She didn't deny it. "I know. That is to our eternal shame. With those harsh words, we lost so much. We lost you, and we lost our grandson. There has not been a day gone by that we haven't regretted our actions that day." She stepped forward as if she was going to take Keira's hand.

Keira shrank back, bending her body into Jake's.

The woman understood. "I know what we did was wrong. We are so sorry. We wanted to find you to make it up, to tell you of course you always had a home with us."

Every fibre of Keira's body spoke disbelief.

"Our quick words sent you away, and we had no way of taking them back. I can't expect you to forgive us. But we would like to see you, to see our grandson."

Jake thought the woman looked like an abandoned puppy dying for a pet, some attention, but expecting a blow.

She pulled a crumpled piece of paper from her pocket and thrust it at Jake. "Here. Will you take this? Please?" To Keira she said, "It's our address and phone number. I know you'll need to think about it but call anytime. Anytime at all."

Chapter Thirty-Three

Abigail, bless her, knew exactly what to feed a little boy. Hot dogs, the kind where you slather on your own choice of condiments, plus baked macaroni and cheese with three kinds of cheese, Dijon mustard and bacon pieces.

"Is this it? We're *all* supposed to eat *this*?" Mason pushed his plate away.

"Yes." Goodness, thought Adele. Who was the child here? "We're eating a meal that your *son* will enjoy. A way to welcome him to our home."

Mason picked away at the mac 'n cheese, first scooping out all the pieces of bacon.

Paying no mind to his father, Daniel made neat, even squiggly rows of first mustard, then ketchup along the length of his wiener before enfolding it in the homemade bun. Likely these were not the wieners he was used to getting from a grocery store, but they'd still fall into the category of hotdogs. Abigail would never allow ordinary wieners into their kitchen. Probably neither would this child's mother if she knew what went into common wieners, or if she had the means to purchase the quality Abigail shopped for.

Still, the child was eating, which was a good sign that he was settling in. As for the older child, Mason, well, he had on his face what we would call a pout if he was ten.

Poor Missy. She had her worries about her grandchild, as well. It wasn't just her own Annette. Both women had made mistakes when raising their grandchildren. Perhaps grandmothers were not meant to take on the entire task of nurturing successive generations.

It was done now. All they could do was to shore up the family they had and to help Annette and Mason shoulder their responsibilities. Maybe this child of Mason's was the best thing to happen to the pair, force them to grow up and think beyond themselves. At least for the sake of the child, she hoped this was so.

Settling herself in her favorite chair in the drawing room, Adele pulled out her knitting. She was working on a mauve cashmere tam and scarf set.

Movement near the door caught her eye. Daniel. By himself. "Where's your dad?"

A shrug.

Did that mean he didn't know where his dad was or *who* his dad was? Imagine. A child of seven only meeting his father for the first time.

How that pained Missy. To know that her grandson had created a child, then abandoned the babe and mother. They weren't wealthy, but surely there would have been some way to help support the pair financially, even if Mason had not felt he could step into the father's role.

This skated far too close to how both Annette's and

Mason's parents had responded to parenting. Perhaps the grandmothers had been too willing to step in, to take over the reins of day-to-day care while the parents played. Because yes, played was what they did, the four of them.

And Annette and Mason carried on with that tradition. Well, all that would change now with the addition of Daniel. Yes, they would change, if for no other reason than that money meant a great deal to them both, and without a family, Annette would not inherit all that she felt entitled to.

Entitled. How it had wounded Hubert to realize that the son they had raised acted like an entitled brat. Jason was the first in a long line of Henrys to shy away from work. And responsibility. They'd had a glimmer of hope when Jason took up with Rachel, a pleasant girl from a strictly middle-class family, who had always had to work for a living. Rachel even had part-time jobs during high school. Maybe she was just what Jason needed.

Alas, Jason was the stronger of the two, pulling Rachel into his way of life, not the other way around. Within their first year of marriage, Rachel divested herself of any work ethic, any pretense of furthering her education, of having a career. The world was their playground, and they never let baby Annette stand in the way of their fun. Yeah, and see where that had gotten them - early, snowy graves.

Annette was all Adele had left now.

A tug on her knitting brought her back to the present. My, how her mind could drift these days.

Daniel leaned against her chair, his hands brushing up and down the length of the scarf she had finished so far.

Catching her eye on him, Daniel darted upright, pushing his hands behind his back.

"It's soft, isn't it?" Adele picked up the ball of wool, rubbed in on her own cheek, then passed it to the child. "Feel it," she urged.

Wiping his hands on his jeans, Daniel gently grasped the fluffy ball in both hands and brushed it against his cheek. His eyes glowed as they met hers.

"It's called cashmere." When he seemed interested, she explained. "It comes from goats. Goats have two coats, a coarse overcoat, and underneath is this softer fibre that's made into cashmere wool." What a curious child. Would most seven-year-olds want to hear about this? His eyes didn't leave her face. "Maybe I'll find a book about this, and we can read it together." That brought a smile.

Ah, it was going to be nice to have a child around the house again, a child not jaded or spoiled. But if Annette was spoiled, who was to blame? Never mind. She had another chance with this boy in front of her.

"One."

Had he spoken? That was the first thing she'd heard him say all day. "Pardon?"

"One." Daniel pointed to the needle in Adele's right hand, then mimed putting it into wool.

Oh, she got it. "Does your mother use one needle?"

He nodded.

"That's called crocheting. You use one needle for that. What I'm doing is knitting, and it takes two, sometimes even more."

Daniel pushed closer, watching her idle needles.

"Want to watch me knit?"

He nodded, then smiled at her, the first genuine smile she'd seen from the child. She hadn't lost her touch with children. Parts of her mind, yes, but thankfully, this part still functioned. At least for now.

Daniel watched her fingers fly, adding stitch after stitch, row after row. She kept to simple patterns now, none of the laces, cables and twists she used to do. No, as long as she stuck to knits and purls, her rows remained straight and true. Daniel seemed to find it fascinating, nonetheless. It felt good to have someone find her competent. She'd relish this for as long as it lasted.

Daniel leaned more heavily against her knee and yawned.

What time was it? How long had he been here watching her knit? She could get lost in the flick and click of her needles; apparently, he could too.

But where was his father? This was supposed to be their bonding time - space where Mason could grow into his role as father. For this dear child's sake, he had better step up and soon.

She picked up the phone that was ever by her side and pressed 1. Almost immediately, Abigail answered. "Abigail, would you mind sending Mason here, please? I think it's his son's bedtime. Thank you."

Over the next five minutes, Daniel slumped lower until his head rested on her knee. Dear boy. She stroked his hair.

"Yeah, what do ya want?" Mason broke their silence. He appeared in the doorway, his hair flattened on one side.

"I think your son is sleepy."

"Okay." He frowned and turned away.

"Mason." She needed to use *that* tone with him, even though he was well into his thirties. "Your son needs you to put him to bed."

"We showed him where his bed is earlier. If he gets lost, Abigail can show him."

"No!" This was so not the way they were going to start their family life. "He needs his father to put him to bed. You remember the bedtime routine when you were this age - a bath, a snack, and a story before being tucked into bed with a hug and a kiss."

"Me? You expect *me* to do that stuff? Annette said we'd have servants to do the work."

"*Staff* might help, but parenting is a hands-on responsibility. Children need their parents, not people paid to care for them." Please God that she would be well enough for some time to help guide Annette and Mason into doing right by this precious little boy.

During this exchange, Daniel had stiffened and withdrawn. Gone was the relaxed, drowsy lad and in his place, a tense boy with clenched hands, stood erect on his toes.

"Oh, come then, let's get this over with." Mason strode into the room, reaching for Daniel's hand.

Daniel backed up, knocking into a table, toppling a vase. Silence followed the sound of fine china smashing into irreparable splintered pieces.

"See? See what you've done now. Have you any idea how much that was worth? Did your mother not teach you how to behave in someone's house?"

"Mason! That's enough." How could he use that tone with a frightened, small child? "It was an accident. The child is in a strange place, with people he's not known for long. He needs your patience and understanding, not your rebuke." Goodness, how could he not know that? Did he not have a paternal bone in his body? This was his flesh and blood, even if he'd ignored him for all the seven years of his young life.

Daniel, if possible, rose even higher on his toes. Every sinew in his body tightened until the cords in his little neck stood out. So different from that relaxed child almost asleep against her knee.

Mason took another step toward his son. "I'll get him out of here." The roughness in his voice would put anyone off.

From Daniel's mouth came noises. Hard to describe noises. More garbled than shrieks, not quite croaks. But oh, yes, they were sounds of distress, acute distress.

With a glare at Mason, Adele used both hands to hoist herself to her feet. It took a few seconds to find her balance, but then she could move, move towards the child whose anguish was clearly too much for one little body to contain.

Realizing that her knitting was still in her hands, she used that. Approaching him slowly, she gently brushed the half-finished scarf down his arms, one, then the other, over and over. Gradually, the keening noises stopped, and he came down off his toes.

"Mason, go get the car. This child needs to be with his mother tonight." To Daniel, "Is that what you'd like?"

Daniel nodded, then pushed his face into her skirt. She continued to stroke his skin with the cashmere.

"No way. He can't learn that all he has to do is squawk and he can run back to his mother. That won't work when he'd be here for good. He'll have to learn to suck it up." Under his breath he added, "And do it quietly, or I'll shut him up."

Adele was not sure she caught that last part, but she didn't like the look on Mason's face. "We'll work toward permanent, but we have to build up to it. Make him feel safe and secure here, welcomed. Change is hard for children and it's up to us to pave the way. For tonight, it's been enough. Take him back to his mother now."

"This wouldn't be happening if Annette was here. I told her to be back, but oh no, she had stuff to do."

As Mason strapped Daniel into his booster seat, Abigail

appeared at his side with Daniel's backpack. "Here. The boy will want this."

Alone, Mason's last words echoed through Adele's mind. True. Annette should have been here. But would things have gone differently with her presence?

Chapter Thirty-Four

The ride home from Char Cut Roastery was silent. The aroma of the charcuterie less thick than the emotions filling the cab of the truck. Keira rested her head against the cool glass of the side window.

It was enough to have told Jake about the empty chairs and celebrating the birthdays of her dead sisters. That, on top of missing Daniel, was enough.

Then for her mother to appear, after all these years.

Her soul could only take so much.

She'd thought she was tough, had had to be, pregnant and alone. But she'd made it, she and Daniel, and they'd built a good life together.

Now, Mason suddenly appearing, then the memories, and finally her mother. It was like the past hurtled at her all at once. How much could one woman stand?

A lot, the other side of her brain said. A lot. She'd done it before, and she'd do it again. She had to. There was pressure on her hand as Jake squeezed it, then turned it over, lacing their fingers together.

Despite everything, she smiled. She'd lucked out with this man. If worse came to worst, and she had to take Daniel and flee, she'd miss Jake. Terribly.

Her phone trilled. She was not up to dealing with anything more today. A mother first though, she checked the number. Mason!

"Hello?"

"I'm bringing Daniel home. He's upset."

"What happened? What did you do?"

"Sheesh, Keira. Why does it have to be something I did? I wasn't even near the kid when he started up. Adele says that overnight might have been too much for the first time. I was all for making him stick it through, but she said I should bring him back to you and try it again another time." He didn't add that the kid wouldn't shut up. "We'll be there in about fifteen minutes."

Relaying the message to Jake, he said it was good they'd gotten the larger charcuterie.

Walking back to the car, Jake asked, "Wanna talk about it?"

Keira didn't pretend she didn't know what he was talking about and just shook her head.

"She didn't look that scary." Or crazy, he didn't add. No empty highchairs trailed her, at least. He pulled the crumpled note with the woman's address. "Want this?"

Keira shook her head. "Throw it away."

He stuffed it back into his pocket. You never knew…

Mason wasted no time dropping Daniel off. No explanation of what happened, other than Adele told him to bring the child back.

A sleepy Daniel picked away at the food platter until Jake held out his arms. "Ready to go to bed, bud?"

Daniel went to him, laying his head on Jake's shoulder as the big man picked him up and carried him to bed.

No bedtime story this time. The kid was out as soon as his head hit the pillow.

"I thought you grew up in San Jose."

"I did."

Jake pulled the paper from his pocket. "The address your mother gave is for a place in La Jolla."

"Let me see that." Keira took the page and frowned. "They must have moved. Didn't think they'd ever leave that house with its shrine to their two lost daughters."

"*Three* lost daughters," Jake corrected.

"Yeah, riiiight."

"She looked kinda sad. And lonely."

"*I* was sad and lonely when I was pregnant and alone."

Jake hugged Keira to him. Never. Never again would she feel alone if he had any say in the matter. But something about this woman, Keira's mother, bothered him. "She seemed sincere."

"They both did at the time, too."

"I believed her when she said she's sorry."

"And I believed them when they told me they never wanted to see me again."

Keira rested her head on the arm of the sofa while Jake gave her a foot massage. "Change is tough for autistic kids. When he doesn't know what to expect, I can see the anxiety rise in Daniel."

"Today must have exhausted him."

"Me, too." Keira stifled her yawn. "Mason's not giving up, though, is he?"

"Doesn't sound like it. It's on again for next weekend." He felt her foot stiffen under his hands. "Hey, loosen up. You've got a week to prepare for this."

"It's just the thought of him not being with me..."

"Daniel spends time often at Elizabeth or Cynthia or Anna's. Think of this as just another set of adults who love him."

"But those other people don't stake any claims on him. They know he's mine."

Jake squeezed the foot he was rubbing. "Ours."

"Yeah, Daniel's claimed you, hasn't he?" Keira sat up. "It doesn't matter. Mason's not a long-haul kind of person. He'll soon lose interest. He and his girlfriend will have a child of their own and forget all about Daniel."

Chapter Thirty-Five

Annette turned back from the dark window. Brooding is what Gran would call it. "He's weird, you know."

Mason lifted his attention from the screen and his Xbox controller. "Who?"

"Your son. Who do you think I'm talking about?" Sometimes Mason was too dense for words.

"*Our* son, you mean. You've got to start thinking of him like that if we're to pull this off."

Yeah, they needed to pull this off. Everything rested on it. But why did it have to hinge on kids? Damn great-grandfather for making that ludicrous will.

Kids. Like a constant pin prick, or some days more like a knife twisting into her side. Reminders of what was lost to her. Just because of one stupid mishap when she was barely more than a kid herself and now she could never have a child of her own.

Instead, this kid of Mason's would have to do. Who knew that he'd be a defective kid at that? Mason had mentioned nothing about the kid being weird.

That kid creeped her out. Silent, sneaking around. Watching, judging with his eyes, but not saying a word, not one single word.

This time, Daniel knew what to expect.

Mom bugged Mason until he emailed pictures of the house and the people who lived there. Mom made them into a book, and they talked about each room, and the people he'd see there. It was better than going in cold like last time.

Besides, the old lady there was nice and had such soft wool. She said he could call her Grandma. He'd never had a grandma. Neither had Timothy before his mom and Brendan got married, but now Timothy liked having one. She made cookies for him. Cookies were good.

Now Mason was here again, to take him for the weekend. Mom said that this time he was staying overnight and sleeping in the bright yellow car bed. It would be fun, she said. He'd see.

The lady in the apron, Ms. Abigail, greeted him at the door again. Her smile was okay, and she smelled like baking. Maybe something chocolate, like brownies.

Oh, no. The stinky lady walked down the stairs. Maybe she wasn't stinky today, at least he couldn't smell her from here. She showed too much of her teeth when she smiled. She kept coming closer and closer. Now her smell was clear. It was a different one than before, different too than the lingering odor in her car.

Daniel backed up as Annette came right up to him, invading his personal space. He stretched out an arm. At school they taught that was the way to mark your territory - anything within arm's length was personal space and others should avoid coming that close. Everyone knew that, everyone except this Annette person.

She scrunched down beside him, both her knees to one side. She put both of her hands on his cheeks and patted them.

Daniel jerked his head away. He tried to take a step backwards, but Mason was in the way. Sandwiched between the two, there was no escape. His hands came out to his sides and his hands flapped. The fingers of his left hand tangled in the stinky lady's long hair. When he pulled his hand back, some of her hair came with it.

"Ow! The little bastard pulled my hair. Mason, do something about him!"

"Annette, enough." The rebuke came from the old lady standing in the doorway to the drawing room. "No language in front of the child. He didn't mean to pull your hair; it was an accident." She came forward slowly. "You frightened him."

The old lady stopped a few paces away. "Remember me, Daniel? I'm your Grandma Adele." She smiled, a real smile, with just the right amount of white teeth showing. She smelled, too, but just a little bit, and it was a nice smell, a warm one. Maybe a bit like a flower.

He wanted to force a word out, but none came. He used a bit of a smile instead, and that seemed to satisfy Grandma Adele. He checked her hands. Yep, in her right one was the mauve yarn. He went to touch it, his hands remembering just how soft it was.

"Oh, yuk," said Annette. "He's putting his grubby hands all over your wool." Then to Mason, "You'll have to teach your son what he can and cannot touch."

"*Our* son," reminded Mason.

"Mason, take the child's things up to his room," said

Grandma Adele. "And you, little man, come along with me. Ms. Abigail has made something special for you. Can you smell it? I think the brownies must be out of the oven now."

She was right; they were. Perched on high stools at the center island, they sat to munch what was on the plates set before them. A glass of milk for him, and a glass of some golden liquid for Grandma Adele.

"Mason, Annette," called Grandma Adele, "come play with your son."

"I'm busy," came the stinky lady's voice. Then to Mason she said, "Your kid. You go."

"I'm doing this for you, you know," Mason reminded her.

"And yourself. Don't pretend you haven't gotten used to all this." She waved her hand around at the opulent suite.

Muttering under his breath, Mason entered the drawing room.

"Did you remember what we bought for Daniel?" Grandma Adele's chin pointed to a cabinet.

"Oh, yeah." Reaching, Mason pulled out a new Lego kit. "Here. Have at it, kid."

"Thanks." There. That word came out all right. Mom would be proud.

Grandma Adele interrupted him to say it was dinner time. Mom usually gave him a five-minute warning before he had to stop playing. Maybe Grandma Adele didn't know about that. He held up all five fingers to show her.

"What a rude little boy," said Annette. "Did he just tell you to wait five minutes?"

"I don't think he meant it rudely," her grandmother said. "Watch him. Let's time this and call his name in another five minutes."

"I never remember you catering to *me* that way when I

was his age." It looked like the stinky lady was pouting. Mom never liked it when he gave that look.

"Okay, it's been five minutes, Daniel." Grandma Adele stood. "Mason, take him to wash his hands."

"The kid knows the way. I've shown him several times now."

Daniel left the room and went to the lavatory down the hall.

Dinner was homemade, oven-baked fries and chicken nuggets, but neither tasted like what he got at McDonald's. The stinky lady complained about the meal, but really, it tasted pretty good.

After eating, the lady took her glass tinkling with ice cubes and her smell with her up the stairs. Mason followed her. Grandma Adele just sat.

Well, Lego awaited.

It sounded like a chair toppled over. Did that come from back in the dining room? Silence, then maybe a sob.

Sobbing meant sadness. It wasn't good to feel sad.

Edging around the doorway for a look, the hallway remained silent and empty. Only a faint odor of the stinky lady remained.

There. That sound again. Maybe from the dining room.

Peeking in, there was Grandma Adele, but she looked funny. No longer standing straight, but her head bowed, sort of shrunk in on herself. Her hands clasped each other over and over, rubbing each other. And those sounds came from her.

Why was she sad? Lonely that Mason and the stinky lady had left her all by herself? No, that couldn't be it. It was good to be away from that Annette. She didn't act like she liked any of them.

Gently reaching out, he touched the elderly woman's hand. Grandma stopped her rubbing and her noises and looked at him, but looked at him funny. Scared. Her eyes wide and kind of wild, like she didn't know who he was or where she was. But this was her house.

It might be her house, but not the room where she liked to sit. Grasping her hand, he pulled. Her feet shuffled after him, letting herself be led out of the dining room and down the hall.

Behind them, someone entered the dining room. "Goodness. What happened here? Why's the chair on its side?" Footsteps, then Ms. Abigail was there. "What are you…? Oh, no." Abigail watched as Daniel led Adele, painfully slowly, step by step, down the hallway toward the door to the drawing room.

Grandma Adele made noises, fretting-like sounds. That was okay. It was sometimes extra hard to get proper words out when upset. She'd feel better soon.

Slowly, slowly, they made their way until they were beside the gold, comfy wing chair. Placing one of her hands on the padded armrest, Grandma Adele got it, and lowered herself onto the seat with a sigh.

Her hands grasped the ball of wool he placed on her lap. With his guidance, her hands stroked the soft skein, over and over. Her noises slowed, then stopped.

Daniel climbed into the big chair, squeezing himself alongside Grandma Adele, the two of them cocooned together, gently brushing the knitted scarf and the ball of wool.

From the vantage point of the doorway, Abigail watched as the little boy instinctively seemed to know what would soothe Adele. The Missus was calmer now, with the small child pressed close to her side, both of them stroking the wool. She backed out to make a call.

"Mrs. Tait? It's Abigail. I think you'd better come. She's had another episode." She listened. "No, Annette and Mason weren't around. Just their son." She waited. "Yes, he's fine. In fact, he's better than fine. He helped her. But she'd not out of it yet, and I might need help if the other two come downstairs." Quieter now, "I think these spells are becoming more frequent."

Chapter Thirty-Six

Abigail rapped on the door to the foyer of Annette's and Mason's suite the next morning. "Excuse me, but Mrs. Henry requests your presence in the drawing room for a family meeting."

Annette flopped back onto the bed. "Oh, not again. Stuff of my nightmares."

"What do you mean?" Mason asked.

"All the time I was growing up here, Gran would call these 'family meetings'. They were usually an excuse to rag on me about something. I'd broken something, I hadn't cleaned my room, although we had enough servants to do it. Later, it was because I'd come home too late or there'd been a call from my school. You name it, she could turn anything into an excuse for a 'family meeting'. Meeting my ass. More like an excuse to rag on Annette."

"So? You're not a kid anymore. What can she do?"

He wasn't the sharpest knife in the drawer, but was he really that dense? "Look around you. Everything you see here is hers. Until I inherit, we depend on her largesse."

Opening the suite door a crack, Mason said, "We'll be down in a bit."

Abigail didn't move. "Mrs. Henry said now."

"Okay. Tell her soon." He shut the door.

"Can you start? I think the wording we worked on is good. Then I'll talk about the power of attorney. We want that clear from the beginning."

Missy squeezed her old friend's hand. "Certainly." Asking for help had never been easy for Adele. This cursed illness had already robbed so much from this proud, brilliant woman and would take even more.

The click, click of Annette's stilettos echoed on the marble floor of the hallway, accompanied by the softer pad of Mason's sneakers. The pair appeared in the doorway.

Not for the first time, Missy wondered what Annette saw in Mason. Of course, Mason was her grandson, the child she'd raised, and she loved him dearly. But right now, his appearance made him less than endearing. Grey, low-slung sweatpants, with fraying cuffs. Unlaced, high-top trainers. A thinning t-shirt that was once probably black clung to his shoulders. Not bad shoulders, but they'd show to better effect without three days' worth of scruff on his chin and an acute case of bed head.

In contrast, Annette appeared dressed for a day's shopping on Rodeo Drive, or as if she'd just returned, sporting her new wardrobe. Not one hair out of place, not one blemish on her glossy fingernails.

Whatever did she see in Mason? Sure, they'd grown up together, play pals as children, but now? The contrast was never as marked as it was today.

Annette gracefully lowered herself to one end of the

love seat, skirt rising to a precise height on her toned thighs as she crossed her leg, one shiny pump dangling from a high arch. Trailing a step or two behind, Mason flopped onto the love seat, taking up more than half of the space with his widespread, gangly legs, and his hips slouched low on the cushion.

Missy cringed at first the sight of her grandson, then at herself. She'd grown up in the house, a child of the house-keeper, but best friends with the manor-owner's daughter. Yet the Henrys had never made her feel second class. *They* knew what class was.

What was wrong with her, feeling shame at her grand-son's appearance? He was a good boy, a nice man. The fact that outward appearance meant nothing to him was a good feature. He was content in his own skin, even if that skin had not seen a shower yet today.

Adele, sweet Adele, looked at Mason kindly, and for that, Missy was grateful. Adele believed he'd be a settling influence on Annette. Maybe. Missy was less confident.

But doubts were useless now. Their path was set and there was no time for a Plan B.

"Annette, Mason, thanks for coming," Missy started. "Annette, a while ago your grandmother told you about the inheritance terms of the will."

"Yeah, Grandma, we got it. I'm working on it. The kid will be here again this weekend."

"That's good, but that's not what I mean, Mason." She took a shaky breath. "Adele asked me to give you some news. Some not very good news."

"About the money?" asked Annette. "I know the econo-my's gone to shit, but I thought our investments were protected."

Adele scowled at her granddaughter. "Not everything is

about money." Although wasn't it? Isn't that the whole reason for this plan? She looked at Missy.

"The inheritance requires that you have a family, yes. But I'm afraid the timeline might need to be moved up." She felt Adele's eyes on her. "No, not might. It *will*." Clearing her throat, she leaned forward to touch Annette's hand. "I have some bad news for you. It's about your grandmother."

All eyes swivelled to Adele.

"Adele is ill. And yes, she's seen doctors, the best in the field, but she has a condition that is worsening." This was the hardest part. "She has a brain condition. It affects the frontal and temporal lobes of her brain, and it's getting worse."

Annette's brows furrowed. "You *look* okay," she told her grandmother.

"Outwardly, she has not changed. It's internal, affecting her brain. Although it's always fatal, some people live with this condition for years, but in some it progresses rapidly. In Adele's case, it's the latter." Her voice broke.

Mason had the grace to look at least somewhat concerned. After all, this woman had been like a second grandmother to him growing up. "How long do you have?"

Adele shrugged. "No one knows. Months? Weeks?"

Silence.

Missy couldn't go on.

Adele was always made of stern stuff. "Because this is the brain we're talking about, the effects of the disease are unknown." A little white lie, but the kids did not need to know that. "As a precaution, we've worked with our lawyers. Missy has my Power of Attorney. That means that if I am not able to make decisions, she has control over my medical decisions, my living situation, and all my finances. She will run this household if I cannot."

"How will we know if you're unable to?" This from Annette. "And why her? She's not even family. I'm your granddaughter and your only living relative. Shouldn't that be *my* job?"

Adele shook her head. Rather than saying she didn't trust her granddaughter, the child she had raised, better to blame their forbearers. "It's wrapped up in the will I told you about." This was tiring, more so than she'd expected. "There will be some changes around here that Missy will tell you about."

"Starting Monday, a nurse will move into the suite beside Adele's. For now, just one shift a day, but eventually that will increase to round-the-clock help if the need arises. We didn't want to burden you young people with physical care, and Abigail has enough on her plate already."

"That would be like three people. Is it really necessary to increase our staff by that much?" Now that inheritance was a stone's throw away, Annette worried about squandering money that could be put to better use. "Would it be more economical, and, of course, more comfortable, Gran, if you moved to one of those places specifically for situations like this? Like a really nice hospice, or something? With people who understand your needs?" Rather than turning this house into a hospital. Visions of nurses in white, starched uniforms and caps with crepe shoes, silently policing the hallways.

Adele raised her chin. "I have chosen to remain in my home and have the space and means to do so. If that was to change in the future, it would be a decision entrusted to Missy."

Annette eyed Missy. She'd always been soft, even when they were kids. She could be managed.

Missy and Adele locked gazes, both reading Annette's mind.

Adele's smile was wry. Little did Annette know of the fibre in Missy's spine. She'd learn, though soon enough.

"Adele has another round of neurological assessments lined up in two weeks."

Mason sat up, at least a little straighter. "Do you need someone to go with you? Drive you?"

Bless the boy. At least she hadn't totally screwed up his upbringing. "Thank you, but no. Oliver will drive us, and I will accompany Adele to the appointments, not just as her friend, but as her Power of Attorney."

"We expect that shortly after that, the team of neurologists will declare that it is time to invoke the Power of Attorney."

Annette frowned. "Shouldn't that be my job? I mean, I *am* your blood relative and all."

"No, I have chosen, and it's done." Adele could adopt a patrician voice when needed. "But this affects you." She looked at the young people on the love seat. "Both of you. Missy will explain."

"Remember the terms of the will? If the current heir dies or became incapacitated, the estate passes on to the next in line, as long as that person meets the marriage and family conditions of the will." She directed this to Annette. "That would be you. But you're not married, nor do you have a family at the moment."

That made Mason sit up. Now the implications were sinking in. "But I'm bringing Daniel here, every weekend now."

Adele shook her head. "That's not enough."

"Mason, he's *your* son. That doesn't help Annette. For Annette to inherit, she must be married and have a family."

Annette turned to her boyfriend. "We could fix that. The marriage part, at least." Turning to her grandmother, "Would that work? If we got married, would that count?"

"It would help. But a family is more than a one-night-a-week affair. There should be a paperwork trail. You should have a copy of the child's birth certificate, a passport, things like that. You'll have to be able to prove to the courts that you're a family. The child must live here with us."

Chapter Thirty-Seven

Something crunched in Jake's coat pocket. Reaching in, he pulled out a crumpled piece of paper. Smoothing it out, he remembered. The note Keira's mom had passed to them, the one Keira didn't want to keep.

Just in case she changed her mind one day, he should put it some place safe. On her kitchen wall, near the back door, Keira kept a bulletin board. There. That was a good place for it. Rearranging notices, he used two thumbtacks to attach the note to the board. Then, for good measure, he used his phone to take a picture of it. You never knew...

"Keira, I've been thinking."

Keira tucked her feet to the side on the love seat and turned to face Jake.

"One of the guys at work took his family on a vacation and he can't stop talking about it."

"Where'd they go?"

"It's called Beaches on Seven Mile Beach, near Negril, Jamaica. It's part of the Sandals chain, but for families. He talked about it so much, I looked it up online."

"Look good?"

"Does it ever." He took a sip of his beer. "I've been thinking. This stuff with Mason has been hard on all of us. When things settle down, why don't we take Daniel and go there for a holiday?"

"Do you think it would suit him?"

"Yeah, I do."

"Okay."

"That easy?"

"Yep."

"There's more."

"Is this the 'but'?"

"Not necessarily. Brendan has heard these same stories over and over about this place. He told Elizabeth and they're wondering about taking Timothy there."

"That might be fun if we all went together."

"Exactly. My passport's good for a few more years. Yours?"

"Yeah, but Daniel doesn't have one."

"Better apply for it soon. You never know how long things are taking these days."

"Jake, this is strange. I'm applying online for Daniel's passport, but the system won't let me. It says there's already an application in process for an individual with this name, birthdate, and city. Approval is pending."

Gran was going to have a cow when she saw these bills, thought Annette. What could she expect, though? The old lady pushed them to get married right away.

Gone was every little girl's dream of a fairy tale wedding in an elegant chapel with hundreds of guests. There just wasn't time to pull that off, at least in the style fitting of their station.

So, Vegas it was.

There was the cost of flights and hotel rooms for their 50 guests. You couldn't expect people to pay their own expenses when the wedding was sprung on them last minute like this. But they were saving money because most of these guests came as couples, so there were only half that many rooms required. Well, suites, that is. After all, these people were used to the best.

It had to be 50 guests because wedding venues added on a surcharge for fewer guests than that. See, that was another savings.

The wedding dress, well, there was no getting around that. To get something decent, something she'd not be embarrassed to wear, would have been pricey at any time, but to get something rushed like this sent the price up almost double. Couldn't be helped.

Food was the same anywhere. The catering at just under $200 per person didn't really differ from what they would have paid had the event had been catered here at home.

The bar tab would run close to that. They could have compromised a bit, but who wants to toast to cheap champagne?

Details. So many details. The wedding planner was a godsend and absolutely necessary, despite costing as much as the venue fee. Without the planner, it would have been impossible for Annette to have found the time to attend to all these extra things that made a day special.

Only one week to go.

Dinner with Gran was quiet. Some days, the old lady said little. Tonight, though, she had an agenda.

"Have you two thought about names?"

Mason and Annette looked at each other. Was Gran losing it?

"Surnames when you get married. Surely you must have considered this."

"No, we haven't given it any thought. Why?" Mason asked.

"It's traditional for the bride to take the groom's last name, but that doesn't really work in this case, does it? The Henry name is a legacy."

"So?"

"Annette, there is a lot associated with your name and it should carry on. Perhaps you should break with tradition, and have Mason assume your name."

"What's wrong with Tait?"

"I see what you mean, Gran," said Annette. "Maybe something hyphenated, like Tait-Henry?"

Mason considered. "You mean we'd both become Tait-Henry?"

Annette shook her head. "No, I meant just you." Sheesh. What was so special about the name Tait? It didn't mean anything to anyone.

"And there's another thing," said Adele. "What about the child? What name did you use on the adoption petition papers?"

"Tait," said Mason. "He's my son. Currently he goes by Foster, after his mother."

"How many names do you want to saddle the poor child with? Foster? Tait? Henry? Wouldn't it be simpler if all three of you were Henrys?" She set down her fork and rose from the table. "Annette, you might want to discuss this with the lawyers before they draw up your wedding certificate. These decisions have ramifications down the road."

Annette got it. "There are so many pieces to this inheritance thing."

"True," agreed Adele, pleased with her granddaughter. "Each puzzle piece must be correctly positioned if you hope to complete the picture properly. You realize how much is at stake." Placing her napkin on her plate, she stood. "Now, if you'll excuse me...."

Annette left for a pedicure appointment. Alone, Mason slumped with his feet on the Wedgwood coffee table. If his grandmother was here, she'd nag - get your feet off that table, sit up straight, quit moping.... Yeah, he'd heard it all before.

What Adele said about names bugged him. Surely she'd discussed this with Missy. Maybe not, though; Adele was a force and believed that money overrode everything else.

Where did that leave him? Was the only thing he brought to this deal the fact that he'd been a sperm donor? If that was his key to this house and all it meant, he'd need to deliver. Daniel would be his.

Chapter Thirty-Eight

Mason held out his hand to take Daniel's backpack. He didn't really need to since it was lighter now that Daniel had toys and clothes that remained at Mason's house.

It was easier now. The kid didn't look like he was about to be dragged to the lion's den every time Mason picked up his son for the weekend. And Keira didn't look like she battled tears.

"Hey." Mason looked at him in the Maserati's rear view mirror. "Want to grab something to eat?" It was mid-afternoon, and he was starving. They'd had a late night out with friends, so he'd slept in, slept right through breakfast and lunch. That meant no food until dinner, unless he stopped at a restaurant. Stupid rules of Adele's. The kitchen at the mansion was off-limits to the family; it was Abigail's domain. Couldn't even go in there to make himself a sandwich. Annette had no problem with the no-eating-between-meals rule; she'd grown up that way. Besides, if you could exist on lettuce leaves, missing the odd meal was no biggie. But for a guy like him…

What was the point of having staff if you couldn't tell them to make you a snack? Adele said Abigail and the kitchen help had too much to do to be catering to the family in that way. Well, she'd be gone soon, and he'd make changes then.

In the meantime, his stomach protested.

There was no sound from the back seat. Of course not. He checked the mirror, caught his son's eye, and asked again.

Daniel nodded enthusiastically.

Okay, so maybe communicating with the kid wasn't impossible. "I know a place with good hotdogs and poutine, a quiet place." Not Chuck E. Cheese. No, he'd learned that lesson.

Thankfully, the kid could read. How had Keira managed this before then? How did you guess what a kid wanted in a restaurant if he wouldn't speak? *Couldn't*, he corrected himself, hearing Keira's impatient explanations in his head. Not speaking wasn't a choice Daniel made, she told him over and over. Weird, but okay, if that's how they wanted to play it. They needed a kid, and this kid was it.

When the server came, Daniel pointed on the menu to a small poutine and a plain hotdog, and a malt shake. Mason ordered the foot-long chili cheese dog with onions, regular poutine with bacon, and black coffee.

One thing about this place was that it was fast. It'd been a while since he was here because Annette hated it. Fat, and carbs, and calories - all the good stuff that she refused to eat.

At least there was no need to try to make small talk with the kid while they waited. He'd barely checked his messages before their food arrived. The kid's plates looked barren compared to his, but that's what Daniel chose, so he'd have to live with it.

Daniel stared at the gloopy mess Mason bit into, watching the drips roll off the sides and onto the plate. How could anyone eat such a tangle of foods, all smashed together?

Carefully he made two exact lines down his own wiener - one bright red one of ketchup, and a glistening yellow one of mustard. No onions, no relish, and certainly no chili. Chili was a separate meal. Why would you throw chili on top of a perfectly good hotdog?

Fascinated, he watched Mason tuck into his food. Wow, he could open his mouth wide. Ew, gross! Sometimes the guy didn't close his lips when he chewed, and the mashed-up bites of food and spit showed through. Mom would never let him eat like that.

The poutine was good, best if you didn't look at it. Poutine was a hard thing. It combined three types of food - fries, cheese, and gravy. Normally, two was the limit for mixing up foods, but with poutine you had to make an exception. If you were really careful, you could fork up bites that had just two things on it - either fries and gravy, fries and cheese, or gravy and cheese. It meant that sometimes you had to brush gravy off a fry with your fork, but it could be done. And it was worth it.

Mason, his dad, didn't know about that. He just forked everything in all at once, sometimes even adding a bite of poutine to the chili dog mess he'd already shoveled into his mouth. Yuck!

The malt was good, although it took some effort to suck the thickness through the straw. He came to an especially hard part, sucking for all he was worth. Slurp! He stopped; cheeks sucked in. Looking around, had anyone heard? Mom wouldn't like this.

From across the table, Mason watched his son over the top of his coffee cup. Slurp. He did it again for good measure.

Had his dad just sucked in his coffee?

There, he did it again. Then he grinned and slurped a third time.

Daniel gave an answering slurp through his malted milkshake.

Chapter Thirty-Nine

"Maybe I ate too much. I don't feel so good." Mason looked at him in the rear-view mirror. "You okay, kid?"

Daniel nodded. A bit full, but he hadn't been able to finish either his malt or poutine. The gross way Mason ate hadn't helped. Mom said you had to chew your food properly. Mason should listen to Mom.

Grandma Adele sat in her favorite chair, knitting. It didn't look like she'd gotten much done since the last weekend he was here. Maybe she just liked to feel the pretty wool running it through her fingers.

Mason slouched on the love seat and didn't even try to join him playing with Lego this time. He just ran his hand over his face, or his stomach, or sighed. That was okay; he wasn't very good at helping build things, anyway. He hogged all the good pieces to himself, rather than trying to build something complimentary to what Daniel was creating the way Jake did. Jake got it.

Suddenly Mason got to his feet, then raced out of the room and down the hall. The bathroom door shut with a bang. Within seconds, gross sounds of throw up came from behind that closed door. Really yucky sounds. Bracing, the smell would come any minute now. But the little room was far enough away, and the stink didn't penetrate the drawing room.

Grandma Adele's needles clicked, clicked away again.

The muffled noise of flushing, then a tap running and running.

Mason returned, flopping hard onto the love seat, taking up most of the space. "I'm sick."

"Could it have something to do with what you drank or the quantity?"

No, Grandma Adele was wrong. He'd seen Mason drink coffee. Mom drank coffee all the time, and it never made her sick. But Grandma Adele hadn't seen all the stuff Mason ate, and the way he ate it all mucked together. That would make anyone barf.

"No. There must have been something bad in the loaded chili dog I ate on the way here."

"You didn't feed that to this child, did you?"

"Relax, Adele. The kid's fine. He had a plain hot dog."

No, not plain. It had ketchup and mustard on it. Plus, there was the poutine and malted shake. Sometimes people were not very precise.

With a groan, Mason ran for the bathroom again.

This time he'd forgotten to close the door and the sounds of retching, violent retching filled the hallway, then the drawing room.

Grandma Adele got up and drew closed the sliding pocket door of the drawing room, somewhat blanketing the sounds of Mason hurling up ground chunks of the food he'd scarfed down.

Bits. They'd looked so gross when Mason chewed them with his mouth open. They'd looked gross even on his plate, uneaten. So many colors and textures and smells all bashed together.

Now they'd look so much worse, coming back up. And the stink. Surely that door wouldn't keep it out, and tendrils of the odor would enter this room at any moment.

"Daniel!" It was Grandma Adele. "Daniel, stop it." She stood right close. "Look at me, just me. Don't think about it. Look at me!"

It worked. It helped. Especially when she handed over the soft, mauve wool to stroke.

The pocket door slid partly open.

"I'm sick," Mason told them. "I'm going to bed."

"Mason." Adele's voice was sharp. "You have company. Your son is here. If you can't be with him, send Annette down. As his parents, at least one of you needs to be with him."

It was nice in the drawing room with just the two of them. Grandma Adele was good at being quiet, sometimes knitting, sometimes just sitting. She never bugged him to talk.

Sometime later, Annette entered the room. She took the seat where Mason had been. Crossing her knees, she rocked one lower leg back and forth. The swish, swish sound of the legs of her pantyhose rubbing against each other filled the silence.

"I made Mason move to one of the guest suites. He stinks, and he was going to ruin my bathroom."

He stank. True. But ruin a bathroom? Even when he'd

been sick and not made it to the toilet, Mom didn't say he ruined anything. It was all cleaned up the next time he entered the room.

"That's fine, dear."

Funny that Annette was so particular about stinks since she stank most of the time herself. Maybe it was different stinks that bothered her. There were definitely differences. Like today. Today she didn't stink quite so badly. It still filled the room, but not the kind of smell that penetrated and filled you up.

"Daniel," Grandma Adele said. "If you check the drawer, there are two new puzzles for you."

She did that every time. Always got a new jigsaw puzzle or two. She was a nice old lady, even if she was a bit funny sometimes. That's okay. Sometimes things were hard for people, Mom said.

Grandma Adele stood up, her knitting falling to the carpet. She just stood there, wringing her hands, and looking around.

"Gran?" Annette looked up from her shiny magazine. She went to the door and called out. "Abigail, get the nurse. Gran looks like she might pass out."

Annette stood by the door until the nurse lady came. Maybe she was afraid her stink would make Grandma Adele worse.

The nurse spoke quietly and took Grandma Adele's hand. Grandma Adele shuffled her feet as she allowed herself to be led from the room.

"This is ridiculous." Annette flounced back in. "She should be in a hospital or somewhere like that. Why should we have to be subjected to scenes like this?" She turned in her seat. "And you. Gran says that when you're here, either Mason or I have to be with you. Mason cooked up some excuse, and now I'm stuck here. It'll be different, you know, when you're here for good. We'll have nannies and stuff so we can get back to our lives."

Whatever. At least the smells wafting around her weren't so awful today.

Supper was quiet, with just the two of them, Daniel and Annette. Only Abigail smiled at him and set a nicely oozing grilled cheese sandwich in front of him, cut precisely in triangles. Nice!

"What's wrong with you, Abigail? Carbs and fat? I can't eat that." Annette's lip curled in a not nice way.

"Your plate will be right out, Miss Annette. A spinach salad with avocado, strawberries and almond slivers, and a honey, balsamic vinegar reduction on the side."

"Well, that's okay, then."

The grilled cheese was good. There was a mix of orange and white cheese in the middle, so with the bread, that meant three things. But the cheeses blended together and tasted yummy, so maybe it was really just two things.

If Mom were here, she'd have something to say to Annette. "Don't pick at your food."

Finally, Annette put her fork down and wiped her mouth with the linen napkin. "I can't hang around here all night. I've got things to do." She pushed back her chair and left. Her high heels clicked on the marble floor, then the carpeted stairs silenced her footprints.

Lego was okay and so were puzzles, but after putting them together twice, where was the challenge? Even Grandma Adele's wool lost its charm.

Wool! That's what Grandma Adele needed to feel better. She'd forgotten it when the nurse led her away. But where was she now?

This place was huge! Like ten times their house. Finding the way around Timothy's house was easy, and so was Amy's. Bonnie's place was bigger, but still not hard. And not silent, never silent like this place.

Home wasn't silent like this, either. The fridge or the air conditioner made noises. Mom's keyboard clicked. And he wasn't alone. She was always there, or Jake was.

Mom. Beside where Grandma Adele always sat was a phone. He'd seen her use it. Not like Mom's cell phone, it had actual buttons to push and a thing you held to your ear. Way back in kindergarten, they had phones like this in the play center. All the kids had to practice punching in their phone numbers on it.

Mom. What was she doing now? Daniel picked up the phone and punched in Mom's number.

"Hello?"

Mom's voice. It sounded so good. "Mom." There, he got it out.

"Daniel? Daniel! Where are you, honey? Is Mason there?"

Her voice sounded funny, that scared, trembly kind of tone. She sounded like that when Amy had gotten stolen last year. No other words would come out, despite so many of them jumbling around in his brain.

Sitting on the chair was the ball of wool. Soft, so soft to stroke. Calming. Grandma Adele needed this, too.

The ball in one hand, the needles and scarf in the other, the carpet silenced his footsteps. Up the stairs, and to the right, were the suite of rooms for Mason and the stinky lady. And him. Maybe Grandma Adele was the other way.

So many rooms, all with closed doors. Was it snooping to open them to try to find Grandma Adele? You're not supposed to snoop in other people's houses. But was that just for closets and cupboards? If Mom was here, she'd know.

In school you're supposed to do things in an orderly manner, like when counting math manipulative pieces. At the far end of the corridor was a door. Begin there.

Stiff latch. Both hands needed. Finally, the knob turned. A staircase.

Downstairs, cleaning up for the night, Abigail noticed the phone by Adele's chair was off the hook. Just one of so many things that Mrs. Henry now struggled with. Things that used to be rote just weren't happening anymore.

Gently, Abigail placed the receiver in its cradle, then turned off the lights in the drawing room and the hallway, shutting the manor up for the night.

Chapter Forty

"Daniel! Daniel, where are you? Can you hear me?" Keira's hand clenched around her cell, straining to keep her voice from trembling. Wouldn't do to frighten Daniel anymore than he already might be. "Say something, Daniel. Or tap the phone."

Nothing. Over the years, there had been times when his inability to speak caused her great grief. Never more so than now.

But they had rehearsed for times like this. He knew how to dial a phone, all sorts of phones. He knew how to send a text message. But with a voice message, they worked out that he would tap the phone - once for yes, and twice for no.

He was doing neither now.

"Jake! Something's wrong!"

Instantly awake from his nap on the sofa, Jake's cop senses tingled. "What? What is it?" He couldn't see anything wrong in the house.

"It's Daniel. He called."

"Oh, that's nice."

"No, Jake, you don't get it. He phoned and said, 'Mom', then there was nothing."

"Is he still on the line?"

"I don't think so. He's not replying or tapping. I can't hear anything."

"Okay. We'll keep your line open. I'll call Mason on my cell."

The call went to voicemail.

"Do you have Annette's cell number?"

Keira shook her head.

"I'll try their house line."

It picked up after three rings. "Good day. You have reached the Henry residence. Staff have retired for the evening and the house phones set to receive voice mail. If you wish to leave a message, we will get back to you tomorrow. If you wish to speak to a family member, please call their private cell number."

Jake fished his keys out of his pocket. "Grab your coat and let's go. I'll drive. Take my phone and leave a message on their house line."

"Jake, there's nothing on my phone now. I think I heard a click, then nothing."

Twenty minutes. Anything could happen to a small boy in that amount of time. A long, long twenty minutes to get there, out of town, through windy forested roads. He wouldn't try to walk home on his own, would he?

Keira peered through the gathering gloom outside Jake's windshield, the tree shadows broadening their grip on the scant remaining light.

Where was Mason? Why wasn't he answering? Why wasn't anyone answering?

Daniel

Neat staircase. It went up, then turned, then turned again. Cool. It went up forever.

A landing, then another door, this one with glass and a bar to push, sort of like the big doors at school. It swung open easily.

Wow!

In the middle was a bubbling tub, way too big to be a bathtub, but too small for a pool. Steam rose into the night air, wafting up and up like smoke. A wide ledge ran around the tub, with pillows and folded towels.

Leaning over, the billowing steam felt fresh, warm, then cooling, with a nice smell. Not like that of the stinky lady, but something nice. Maybe like flowers. The water felt soft, like when Mom put in bath oil. Bubbles rose from the bottom from all over, some faster than others. In one corner was a ladder, like the kind to help you get out of a swimming pool.

Following the steam up into the sky, his eyes saw the inky darkness and the twinkling lights. Wow! It was like that time when Jake took them camping way out of the city and they lay in the grass looking at the stars at night.

Did people sleep up here? There were wide beds with pillows, but no covers, just folded towels. Some of these beds had tilted umbrellas beside them, and little tables. Near the wall was a long counter with a sink, taps, and a fridge.

The other three sides were like a huge balcony with clear glass panels along the edge and a railing on top. In front of the railings were high, narrow wooden tables with stools tucked under them.

The railings were at the wrong height, requiring tip toes to see overtop, or scrunching down to see through the glass. A stool helped, but not enough.

Climbing from the stool to the narrow table was better. Ah, now the view. Higher than the highest treehouse ever, taller than any playground climber, like being a bird flying over the grounds.

From here, the trees looked like those on Bonnie and Jordy's miniature railway set, the bushes no bigger than a marble. Too bad there weren't more lights on down there to see everything. It'd be great in the daylight.

Seated on the narrow table, with legs dangling over the edge into the night, Daniel surveyed the grounds of Grandma Adele's estate. It was so cool being here on top of the roof. He spread his hands out behind him on the table, leaned his head back and stared up at the stars.

Chapter Forty-One

No answer. Jake pounded on the front door while Keira's finger repeatedly pushed the doorbell. Why was no one answering? How many people lived in this place, and there was no one who could answer their phone or the door?

"You keep trying and I'll go around to see if any doors are unlocked." Jake vanished into the dark.

"No luck. Doors and windows locked tight." Normally, he'd think that was a good thing. He'd noted one door that looked like a good candidate if they needed to break glass to get in. "Hang on." Jake remembered something. "Didn't Mason say that the housekeeper and butler lived in a cottage on the property?"

"Yeah. It's probably that place between here and the gate."

"I'll run over there and get them. They must have a key to this place. You keep trying to rouse someone."

It was less than ten minutes but seemed an eternity to Keira waiting at the front door, her voice hoarse from yelling. Who could hear her in a place this big, with walls that must be a foot thick?

An older man and woman came up the drive, slowly, far slower than Jake, but obviously trying. The man was mostly dressed, the woman with slippers and a bathrobe over what looked like flannel pajamas flopping around her legs.

The man got there first. "I'm Oliver." Easing Keira to one side, he inserted a key in the lock. He entered first, going straight to a panel in the closet. Within seconds, the beeping sound stopped.

They'd met Abigail before. She started turning on lights. "The last time I saw the lad, he was here in the drawing room with Ms. Annette." Obviously, they weren't there now, although the Lego pieces spread on the carpet gave evidence of Daniel's presence.

Jake was already taking the stairs three at a time. Opening Daniel's bedroom door, he called down. "He's not here, and the bed is still made."

Keira was already in the playroom next door. "It's empty, too."

"I'll check the kitchen. Maybe the child got hungry and wandered down." Abigail left for the dining room and kitchen.

"Where's Mason?" How could she have entrusted her son to that man?

"He and Ms. Annette share the suite through here." Oliver led the way and rapped on a set of double doors.

They waited. Oliver rapped again. Nothing.

Abigail joined them with no news. "No sign that anyone's been in the kitchen or dining room." Seeing there was no response to her husband's knocking, she strode to a panel on the wall. Pushing some buttons, she said, "Sorry to disturb you, Ms. Annette. Would you come to the door, please? We have a problem."

Finally, the sound of some stirring, then a knob turning. A drowsy woman stood in front of them in a satiny, lacy, short sleepwear set. "What? Abigail, you know you're not supposed to disturb us at night. This had better be good."

Keira pushed forward, using her arm to open the door farther. "Where's my son? Is he in here?"

Annette's nose wrinkled in disdain. "Of course not. What would he be doing in here?"

"Where is he?" Keira grabbed Annette's arm.

Annette shook her off. "How should I know?"

Jake stepped up behind Keira. "You're looking after him. You're responsible. What did you do with him?"

"With him? Nothing." Annette stepped back, trying to close her door. "Go ask Mason, it's his kid."

Jake pushed all the way into the room and called, "Mason! Come out here, now!"

Turning her back on the four who'd invaded her space, she said, "He's down the hall. He said he was sick, and I wasn't having him contaminate my bathroom."

"Follow me," instructed Abigail. "He'll be in one of the guest rooms." On the other side of Daniel's bedroom and playroom, she began opening doors. The odor hit them before they saw the sleeping man in a rumpled bed.

Overcoming his momentary squeamishness at the stench from the man, the bedroom and the attached bath-room, Jake shook Mason's shoulder, none too gently. "Wake up, man. Where's Daniel?"

After Jake continued to try and shake some intelligent thoughts into his brain, Mason half sat up against the head-board. "What?"

Keira's loathing for this man had never been greater. "Daniel. What have you done with him?"

"What? Nothing."

"Then where is he?"

"I was sick. I went to bed. Ask Annette." He tried to settle back under the covers.

Jake grabbed his upper arm and pulled the smaller man from the bed.

Tumbling to the floor woke Mason fully. "What's going on?"

"Daniel phoned me. He just said 'Mom', then nothing. My phone said the number was from this house."

"You wouldn't answer your phone, so we drove over here."

"I'm sick. I think I got food poisoning."

Abigail's brows lowered, and she towered over the goon sprawled on the floor. "You did not! No one has ever been poisoned by my cooking."

Mason ran a hand down his face. "No, not your food. From when Daniel and I stopped for a snack on the way here."

"You gave my son food poisoning! Where is he now? *How* is he? Do you even know?"

"He was fine the last time I saw him."

"How long ago was that?"

"I don't know." He looked at the bedside clock. "Maybe four hours ago."

"Four hours!" So much could happen to a little boy in that time.

"Get up," Jake ordered. "We search the house for five minutes, then we call the cops."

"I know the grounds best. I'll start out there," offered Oliver. "Don't worry. The swimming pool has a locked cover on it. We had it installed when we heard the boy would come here. I checked it myself tonight, and it's in place."

"I'll get all the lights on."

The five of them trooped downstairs. It didn't take long to search the pantry, utility room, kitchen, dining room, lavatory, drawing room, and library. There was no need to try the other wing of the main floor. "I kept it locked when Daniel was around due to all the equipment in the exercise room, billiard room, and theatre," Oliver explained.

Back on the second floor.

"If possible, it would be good if we could avoid waking Mrs. Henry. She's not been well." As Keira opened her mouth to speak, Abigail continued. "But if we don't locate the lad soon, we will, of course."

Turning to face the hallway, she pointed at the closed rooms. "These are all guest suites, four of them between here and Mrs. Henry's suite of rooms." She frowned. "That's odd." She pointed to the far end of the hallway. "There, on the floor. That looks like Mrs. Henry's knitting. It never leaves the drawing room where she works on it." She set off down the hallway. "And that door shouldn't be open. I'm sure it was closed when I shut off the lights up here before I left."

"Where's it lead to?" Jake was already striding that way.

"The rooftop deck."

Jake ran right behind him, Keira.

Around and around, the winding staircase took them up two more floors, hearts pounding from exertion and terror.

Rounding the last stairs, a mother's nightmare in plain view. An open hot tub, steam melting into the night air. "Oh, God, please…"

Focused only on that water, neither of them took in the

rooftop's expansive setting. Empty. No bodies floating in the hot tub's roiling water.

Lifting her eyes, Keira saw him. Perched atop a tall, narrow bar table, resting on his arms, legs dangling over that four-storey drop. "Daniel!" She screamed his name, couldn't help herself.

Lost in his own thoughts, humming a tune, Daniel hadn't heard their approach. Startled at the yell, his one hand slipped off the highly polished tabletop, tilting him to one side, with one hip almost over the edge.

Then muscular arms engulfed him, lifting him, holding him to a chest he knew well. Jake. Daniel wound one arm around Jake's neck and pointed at the sky with his other hand. "See?"

Chapter Forty-Two

It took a lot to unhinge Keira. Yeah, she could get mad, and yeah, she'd defend her son to anyone, but to lose it, truly lose it, just didn't happen.

Until now.

"Mommy?" Daniel patted her face from his secure spot in Jake's arms.

Crying in front of her son was something she did *not* do. But she'd lost control of her body, of her emotions, just like she'd lost control of her son.

Jake pulled her into his embrace, the three of them together, a unit. Safe.

"Did you find him? Is the kid okay?" Puffing, Mason climbed the last steps to the rooftop deck.

"That's it! No more. Desert us and ignore us for seven years, then you say you want him and this, *this* is how you look after him! How dare you? How dare you play with my son's life?"

"Geez, Keira. I was sick. Annette was looking after him. The kid's okay, anyway. No harm done."

"No. Harm. Done. *Right.* And where is this Annette, this caretaker of small boys?" She opened her mouth to finish this, to spew all the venom and resentment bottled up inside for so long.

Jake's arm wrapped around her upper arm and his firm voice spoke into her ear. "Not now, Keira. Not in front of Daniel." He pulled her towards the stairs. "You'll have your chance, but now is not the time. Let's get out of here."

The next morning's mail brought a letter from Attorney Julie Franco. Keira steeled herself to open it, slipping her fingernail under the flap. Ow! Paper cut, ow, ow.

Later, Keira, seated with Jake in front of their attorney's desk, could not believe her ears. "Annette is petitioning to *adopt* my son? How can she *do* that?"

Julie addressed the irate couple. "Ms. Henry can certainly file papers petitioning the adoption. But she cannot legally adopt Daniel without consent from you, the biological and custodial parent."

"How could she even think she could have my son?"

"Money. Her compelling reasons are money. The petition talks about the benefits to the child to be raised in a home of considerable means, and the legacy he will inherit down the road."

Jake scrubbed his face. "If Keira and I combined all our current and future assets, we couldn't hope to compete with the Henry fortune."

"The benefits of wealth are also the foundation of Ms. Henry and Mr. Tait's petition for custody."

"They can't do that, can they?"

Julie shook her head. "Ms. Henry cannot adopt Daniel without your consent. I cannot see the Court awarding them sole custody either, since Daniel has always resided with you, and there has been no question about your ability to parent."

Keira sat back, at least partially appeased.

"But," Julie continued, "they can still request shared custody."

"We came to you this morning to inform you that the pair should have no access to Daniel at all." Keira explained last night's phone call from Daniel, his disappearance, the lack of supervision, and the fact that neither Mason nor Annette had any idea about Daniel's whereabouts while he was supposedly in their care.

Julie made notes. "We'll certainly share this incident with the Court. It's likely not enough to prevent shared custody, though."

"How can that be? They're obviously irresponsible, plus if you'd seen them, they couldn't have cared less."

"The Court might see it that none of us are perfect parents. And, while you've had seven years to grow into the role, Mr. Tait and Ms. Henry are still finding their way."

Julie cleared her throat. "One other thing. It says in the petition that Mr. Tait and Ms. Henry are engaged, and their nuptials will take place soon." She directed her gaze to Keira. "Fair or not, a married couple gives the impression of stability more than a household with a single parent."

Keira bristled. "I am twice the parent either of them will ever be. Ten times…."

Jake interrupted, giving Keira's fingers a squeeze. "If it's marriage that will make the difference, we can do something about that right quick."

Keira's head whipped toward Jake.

"What?" he asked. "Where did you think this was going?" He waved their clasped hands between their chairs. "This might have sped things up a bit, but we were going to get there, anyway."

Julie cleared her throat. "Mr. Dean, that is very noble of you. I cannot counsel you to enter into marriage simply for the sake of securing custody."

"As I said, this was inevitable. We were just taking our time getting there."

"But committing to taking on a child, someone else's child...."

"I love that kid. And I love his mother. If I get Daniel along with her, that's a bonus for me. Kind of like a twofer."

"I'll leave this for the two of you to discuss."

"Something else," Jake reminded Keira.

"Oh, yeah." Fuming about Mason's irresponsibility almost made her forget. "We're thinking of taking Daniel on a trip to Jamaica, so I went online to apply for his passport."

Julie nodded.

"I couldn't. The system wouldn't let me. It says there's already an application in progress for him. I've never applied before."

"Is this something Mason would do?" Julie asked. She made note to look into it.

Chapter Forty-Three

Reassured over the fact that anyone other than the legal guardian applying for a child's passport could be considered fraud, slightly raised Keira's spirits. But there was still so much, so very much to worry about. The pieces seemed to jiggle around, none of them holding still long enough to make sense of them or plan a strategy. They were just drifting in a tide out to the vast ocean, with no plan, and no end in sight.

Normally a patient mother, not so today. Maybe Daniel picked up on her mood, maybe his actions exacerbated her frustrations, but it wasn't working.

"How about I take Daniel to the park? Wear off some energy," Jake offered.

"Yes!" yelled Daniel.

Yes, Keira echoed in her mind. She kissed them both goodbye and relished the solitude of her house.

Two hours about did it for Jake. Less so for Daniel, but he'd played hard enough to leave the park without protest.

Just as well. Jake grew increasingly uncomfortable with the stares of an older woman. She never came too close, just near enough to watch them while keeping her distance. She didn't seem to have any children with her, or anyone else. Odd for one woman to remain in the park for so long. Yeah, she had a Kindle she pretended to read, but her eyes seemed to follow Daniel more than her reading device.

"Come on, bud. Let's see what your mom's up to and if she has any grub ready for us." Glancing over his shoulder from time to time, no one on the streets seemed to take any interest in them. Still, his spidey sense tingled, as Brendan would say....

Keira opened the door, giving each of her men a hug and kiss. They smelled of fresh air and sunshine.

Nudging her out of the way, Jake shut the door hurriedly.

Keira gave him a questioning look.

He shook his head and nodded in Daniel's direction.

"Go wash up, son. We'll eat soon." Keira sent Daniel off, then waited for Jake to explain.

"It's probably nothing, but there was this woman at the park."

"Someone hitting on you?" Keira teased.

"No, an older woman. She just sat on various benches. Whenever we moved to a different section of the park, she seemed to suddenly appear, watching. There was something familiar about her, but I only saw her from a distance."

The doorbell rang.

Checking through the peephole, Jake said, "It's her. That's the same red coat, same woman."

"Let me see." Keira looked, then took a quick step back. "No!"

"What? What is it? Do you know her?"

"Yeah. It's my mom."

The pieces clicked for Jake. He'd only seen the woman once before, in the shady foyer of the restaurant where they'd been ordering their takeout meal. Just a few minutes of interaction, really, and he'd been more focused on how Keira was feeling than committing the woman's looks to memory. He was slipping. As a cop, he usually made an effort to remember faces. No wonder he'd thought she looked familiar. "What do you want to do?"

"I don't know. Why is she here?"

"It's your call, Keira. You can open the door and see what she wants. I can go out and tell her to leave. Or you can ignore her and wait until she goes away. I've got your back either way."

While Keira thought, the doorbell pealed again. "I can't have her stalking Daniel. I'll see what she wants and tell her to leave us alone." She took a deep breath and opened the door, steeling herself against seeing this woman who once meant so much to her. Some of her dearest moments, plus her darkest times, were wrapped up with her mother.

Keira stood blocking the half-open door, the warmth of Jake's chest against her back, his arm around her waist. "What do you want?"

"May I come in?"

Torn, Keira hesitated.

Jake's arm helped guide her backwards just a bit, allowing enough room for Maryanne Foster to enter the foyer.

"Hi, Keira." The woman's eyes drank in the sight of her daughter, so much older and more confident than the girl who'd last graced their living room. "How are you?"

"How'd you find us?"

"I've been hanging out in parks for a while now, thinking that if you have a little boy, you'd bring him to a park from time to time. Since I've seen you twice at that mall, I guessed you must live in this area, so I visited the parks around here. Not every day, but a couple of times a week." She looked at Jake's masked eyes. "Today I got lucky and saw this young man with my grandson."

They all turned at the sound of running steps as Daniel barrelled into Jake, wrapping his arms around the man's legs. Only then did he notice their visitor. He looked from his mom to Jake, a question in his glance.

Maryanne got down on her knees in front of the child. She looked once at Keira for permission, then dove in without waiting for it. "I'm your grandma."

Grandma? Daniel frowned. "Not Grandma Adele."

"No, Daniel," his mom agreed. "This is Maryanne." She swallowed. "Grandma Maryanne."

"Two?"

"Yes, you have two grandmothers."

Holding the wall for support, Maryanne rose to her feet. "I won't bother you anymore today. I just wanted you to know how much we've missed you and would like to see you, would like to get to know our grandson." Something caught her attention. A half-step to the left enabled her to see around Jake, into the kitchen. From that vantage point, she could see the bulletin board and the note with her address and phone number thumb-tacked to the bottom. That brought a smile. "I see you've kept my note. Call whenever you want, and you're welcome to drop in anytime. Anytime at all." Her glance took in all three of them, lingering the most on the seven-year-old boy at Jake's side.

Almost as if the words came from someone else's mouth, Keira asked, "Do you want to come in?"

Maryanne's beam was brighter than any smile Keira had received when giving her mom a painstakingly drawn card for Mother's Day as a child. The woman was in and hanging her coat on the newel post before Keira fully realized what she'd said.

To Daniel, Maryanne asked, "Do you have any games?"

In seconds, Rubik's Race Game claimed space on the coffee table, with Daniel on the floor and Maryanne on the edge of the couch. She had just one question for Keira. "Do you let him win?"

Keira shook her head.

"Good." The rest of her chatter was all for Daniel. "Your grandpa is going to be so jealous that I got to play with you."

"Grandpa?" That was a new one to Daniel.

"Yes. You have a Grandpa Bill. He's most anxious to meet you."

Keira and Jake retired to the kitchen. Perching on bar stools, they could see and hear everything taking place in the living room. Unlike when Daniel was with Mason, neither felt that foreboding worry. Maybe it was because they were right close, supervising what went on. Maybe it was because they instinctively knew that Maryanne would protect this child with her life.

"Could this day get any weirder?" The upheavals of the day exhausted Keira. But this latest intrusion on their lives didn't bring with it the angst all the others had wrought.

Maryanne didn't seem concerned that she needed to carry the bulk of the conversation. Daniel seemed relaxed, smiling at his new grandmother. After several rounds of Rubik's Race Game, Daniel packed it away and returned with Clue Junior, setting up the board without a word.

"I used to play this with your mom when she was a little girl."

Daniel looked intrigued, whether because this woman had played with his mom, or because his mom was ever a little girl.

"Daniel, five minutes until supper."

Daniel nodded.

"We'll each take one more turn, then we'll put it away," said Maryanne.

Despite her grandson's hesitation and the slightly stuck out lower lip, Maryanne kept to what she'd said, and packed away the game. Standing, she asked Daniel, "May I give you a hug?"

He went to his new grandmother, putting his arms around her waist.

When Maryanne looked up at Keira standing in the doorway to the kitchen, she mouthed, "Thank you," then turned away, brushing her eyes with the back of her hand. When she pivoted back, her coat was in her hand, and her eyes were clear. "I have so enjoyed playing with you, Daniel, and I hope to get to do it again soon. Maybe your grandpa can join us next time." She put both arms in her coat. "Now you go wash your hands for supper."

"You're welcome to stay," offered Keira. "It's just soup and sandwiches."

"*Just?*" Jake asked. "What do you mean? *I* made the sandwiches, and they're works of art."

"Thank you, dears, but I've outstayed my welcome,

considering I came here uninvited. I can't tell you how much this has meant to me." She hesitated between going to the door or going to Keira.

Keira's feet appeared stuck to the floor, but her eyes were on her mom.

"Oh, for goodness' sake," said Jake. With one hand on each of their backs, he gently pushed the two women together.

Maryanne left, her steps lighter than before, since almost eight years before. She had walked only about half a block when her cell phone showed an incoming text. Pulling it out, she read:

In case you want my number 629 433-6913. Keira.

It was a start.

Chapter Forty-Four

"What should I do, Jake?"

"It's your call. I support you either choice you make." This was not the usual Keira, the woman who plowed her way through the world, shoving away obstacles, making things work for herself and her son.

"But what should I do?"

"What are the pros and cons? They're your parents and they want to see you and Daniel. You can say no, you can ignore them, or you can say yes, on your terms."

"Jake, they hurt me so bad."

"I get that, babe. I can't see how they could have done that to you, but they did. It sounds like they regretted it and wanted to make it up to you but couldn't find you."

"So they say."

"You're hurt and you have every right to be ticked. The thing is, do you want to hold on to that anger, or could you let it go?"

"I don't know. I never thought there'd be any choice."

"One way of looking at it is that could Daniel have too

many people who love him? Letting your parents in would be an additional pair of hearts he'd hold. Is that a bad thing?"

"Look what they did to me. What if they turned on Daniel?"

"From what I saw of your mom, it doesn't seem likely to me she'd do anything to hurt him. But then, I couldn't see her turning you away, either."

"Well, she did."

"True." They both looked at the paper on the bottom of the kitchen's bulletin board. Several times, Daniel had asked about it. That kid knew every scrap of paper under the fridge magnets, and every notice put up on that board. The explanation that it was the address and phone number for the lady who played Rubik's Race Game with him, Grandma Maryanne, satisfied him.

Jake continued. "A kid can't have too many grandparents. My parents would love to play that role, but they're hundreds of miles away in Texas. He's got Adele now, but Mason hinted that she's not well. There's Mason's mother, but no one mentions much about her. That just leaves your parents."

"He's managed just fine for seven years with no grandparents." She spun the diamond ring on her fourth finger, still not used to its feel. Or what it meant to be engaged to Jake.

Jake massaged her knuckles. "Maybe things don't have to be traditional, kind of like my marriage proposal in front of a lawyer. Maybe Daniel has a series of grandmothers. Maybe he only sees Grandma Maryanne, and not your father. Have you thought of that option?"

"No." She considered that. "I'm hurt and mad at both, but especially my father. He's the one who tossed me out.

Mom just stood there and cried, looking miserable, but she didn't go against him. At least not right then."

Keira looked at her mom's address on the bulletin board. "What if I started with her, just her? She did all right with Daniel here the other day. What if he saw her again, just her? It's easier on him to meet one new person at a time, anyway."

"Your call."

"Mother, this is Keira."

"Oh, my dear!"

Could just a simple call bring that much joy to her mother's voice? "We, I wondered if you'd like to play with Daniel again?"

"*Would* I! We'd both love to."

"No! Not Daddy. I mean, just you. It's, it's easier for Daniel with one person at a time."

A pause. "I understand. Your father will be sad, but we understand. We'll do this whichever way you want."

"Could we bring him over? Now?"

"Of course. Your father's out golfing. He said he'll be back by about four."

"We're on our way."

"Nice place," Jake commented. In the side yard, they could see the beginnings of a climbing gym, similar to the one Jake built in Keira's yard for Daniel. But this one looked like it was going to be bigger.

"I wonder if that came with the house?"

"Possibly, but more likely your dad has started building it for his grandson."

244

"Dad always enjoyed working with wood and building things."

"We're fine here if you two want to take a walk or have some time for yourselves." The ring on Keira's finger drew her eyes. "I don't remember seeing that the last time we met."

Jake took the hand Keira tried to hide behind her back. "It's new. We haven't set a date yet, but it will be soon. I can't wait."

"Grandma," Daniel called. Perched on a stool at the counter, he held onto a large mixing bowl with one hand. His other fist gripped a long wooden spoon. The tip of his tongue protruded from his lips as he concentrated on stirring. It was questionable if as much cookie dough remained in the bowl as it did on the counter.

"I'd better get back to our baking job," said Maryanne. "Here." She pressed a key into Keira's hand. "Your father had this copy made for you last week. He said you're to use it anytime, treat this house as yours."

Backing up, Keira felt for the knob of the front door. This place was a landmine of emotional pitfalls. Never had she been this teary in her life. Well, maybe except for when she was pregnant with Daniel.

Returning home with a plate of warm cookies, Daniel hummed the tune of Paw Patrol from his booster seat in Jake's truck.

———

Several days later. "Keira? This is your mother."

"Hi, Mom. Anything the matter?"

"Yes. Your father said I should phone you right away."

"What's going on?"

245

"A young man came to the door. That Mason, your old boyfriend. He made it sound like he was here for Daniel's sake and for you. He wanted our help in getting you to give Daniel to him - he wants custody. He said that he has so much more to offer Daniel than you ever could. He talked about money, lots of money, and some mansion and an inheritance."

"Oh, no."

"Dear, are you in trouble? Do you need money? Your Dad says we can help you. We can mortgage this house if you need funds, and we have some savings. He says to tell you anything we have is yours. Just say the word."

"No, Mom, I'm fine money-wise. But Mason...."

"Don't worry, your dad threw him out."

"What?"

"Mason seemed determined, and he made threats about taking Daniel away from you if you didn't cooperate. I've never seen your father get physical, not in all the years we've been married. But he did with that young man, threw him right out of the house."

Keira looked at the phone. *Her* dad?

"Now, dear, tell me what's going on. Are you and that dear boy in trouble?"

Chapter Forty-Five

"Mason, did you call the cab?"

"Of course I did. You've only reminded me fifty times. If you're so worried about it, why didn't you phone yourself?"

"I've got so much to do! At least you could help a little. I've planned this whole wedding myself."

"Yes, you made a phone call to the wedding planner."

"Mason, there's no need to be nasty. We're getting married tomorrow and I'm a nervous wreck." She pointed to the five suitcases piled haphazardly by the door to their suite. "Take these down to the front door, will you?"

Sighing, Mason grabbed a case in each hand, schlepping them down the staircase. Passing by the door to the drawing room, he noticed his son playing alone. "Hey, kid. You doing all right?"

Daniel nodded.

Mason headed back upstairs.

Soon, Daniel heard raised voices from upstairs. That wasn't Grandma Adele. The nurse said she was napping. No, that was the stinky lady's voice. And Mason's. Fighting again. Why did they always do that? Mom and Jake didn't.

Mom. This was boring playing alone. At least at home, he knew Mom was close by, even if she was working. Or when he wanted something to do, Jake was always willing to hang out with him. Not Mason.

A car horn honked outside the front door. Did no one else hear that? No footsteps.

Daniel went to the front door and peered out. No peephole in this door, so Mom's rule about always checking first didn't count at this house.

A taxi. Taxis always had that special light on the roof. Taxis took you places, places you wanted to go. The taxi man looked at him. Daniel waved.

Going to the closet, he got his shoes and put them on. Next his jacket.

The taxi man stood beside his car. "Is this ride for you?"

Daniel nodded.

"Just a minute, kid " The driver opened his trunk, then returned with a booster seat he placed in the back seat. "Hop in." He waited until Daniel buckled himself in, then asked, "Where to?"

Although the seat belt hampered things, he got his jacket off and showed the man the label sewn into the neck of his coat. Mom put his address and phone number on the inside of each of his coats.

"Okay, got it." The driver started the car and drove out through the open gates. He radioed his destination to his dispatcher.

"Mason, where's the cab? I thought you said you called for one. We're going to miss our plane."

"I *did* order one. It should have been here ages ago. Maybe it came and got tired of waiting. It's taken you forever to get ready." He stepped out the door. "The gates are still open. He must have come and gone."

Daniel's head drooped lower and lower until he nodded off on the drive. It took forever to get from Mason to his mom's house. But they made it.

"You got money to pay me, kid?"

Daniel shook his head. "Mom." He undid his seat belt and opened the door.

"I've been stiffed before. I'll go with you to the door."

No answer to their knock, although the lights were on inside. After the second knock, Daniel left the porch and squirmed in beside purple salvia plants his mom grew against the house. Inching back out, he brought with him a rock that had a secret door. Reaching into the opening, he retrieved the spare key to the door. The lock was tricky, even though he and Jake practiced it lots of times. But he got it.

"Knock, knock," said the driver. "Anyone home?" Entering a stranger's house with a child didn't seem the right thing to do. "Stay right there, kid. I'll be right back." He went to his car to alert dispatch.

Mom wasn't home. Neither was Jake. Would staying here alone be better than being by himself at Mason's? Maybe.

On the counter were the last of the cookies he and Grandma Maryanne baked. They still tasted good. Very good. Wonder if she'd bake more with him?

There. On the bulletin board was the paper with her address and phone number. Careful. Don't want to rip it. Grandma.

Giving the paper to the taxi man, Daniel climbed back onto the booster seat, buckling himself in.

Reading the paper, the driver made a call. "This is Coastal Cab Company. I picked up a kid here. The address he sent me to had nobody home and no one to pay the fare. The kid's too young to be left alone. He gave me your address and number. Should I bring him to you?"

"Daniel? Is that Daniel?"

"Kid, your name Daniel?"

Enthusiastic nod.

"Yeah, seems so."

"I'm his grandmother. Bring him right here. We'll be waiting and there'll be a bonus for you. Please take good care of him."

This was a longer drive, the streetlights mesmerizing, going on forever.

"Lady, the kid fell asleep in the car. Do you want to get him?"

"Yes! My husband will pay you."

Happy with double the cost of the fare, the driver waited while the old lady and man unstrapped the kid from the booster seat and carried him indoors.

Maryanne made a phone call. "Keira? This is your mother. We have Daniel. He's here."

Chapter Forty-Six

Attorney Julie Franco stood. "I have one final witness, Your Honor."

Who was left, Keira thought? They'd already laid bare her financial information, her education credentials, friends as character witnesses, even representatives from her son's school. That was it in her world.

"I call to the stand Mr. Bill Foster."

Keira watched in disbelief as the back door to the court-room opened and a man walked down the center aisle to take his place beside the Judge's chair. If she had passed the man on the street, Keira might not have recognized her father. In the last eight years, he'd aged far more than a decade. His hair, once silver at the temples, was now solid white. Where once full and wavy, it was now sparse. His gait was no longer that of a middle-aged man, but one of advanced years, one that bore the weight of time.

Yet, his voice was firm as he was sworn in.

Then, with prompting, he began his tale. "My wife and I moved here from San Jose, where we'd raised our daughter. After two heart attacks, I retired from my job. Life and family are too precious to spend time apart."

Heart attacks! When had that happened? Was he all right? From behind her, she felt a hand cup her shoulder. Jake. He must have seen her tensing.

Dad continued. "We bought a place in La Jolla, a nice house with a yard, just a block from the ocean. You know, the kind of place where a boy and his granddad can walk the beach, collect shells, skip stones, and create sandcastles."

He made it sound like they'd purposely moved here to be closer to Daniel. But he had wanted no part of her or Daniel. He'd made that very clear.

"We only have one child; we lost two others. And so far, our one child has only has one chick herself. You know how a mother hen is with her one chick. My wife wouldn't rest until we were closer to our daughter and grandson."

He made it sound like they had a relationship, that they were a normal family. Her dad, her straight-arrow father - was he telling a lie? Fibbing to help her case? Perjuring himself? Would he do that for her?

"Mr. Foster," interrupted Ms. Franco. "You're painting an idyllic family picture. Has it always been that way between you and your daughter?"

"No, sadly, it has not." He looked over at Keira, having evaded her direction so far in his testimony. "It wasn't good for a long time and that is all on my shoulders. All of it." He turned back to the attorney. "You see, I'm a stubborn old man. I had this ideal of what my family would be like. Keira was born to us, the most perfect child anyone could ever wish for. Then we were blessed with a second daughter, Jackie. When she was two, she contracted meningitis and died. Were we over-protective of Keira after that? Likely, but you can understand, I'm sure. Maryanne found it hard to let Keira out of her sight when it came time for school, but we worked our way through that. Then my wife found she was expecting again. We were so pleased to bring another sister to Keira. But that child was stillborn."

He pulled a handkerchief from his pocket and wiped his eyes. "Those were hard times for us, but we were blessed to have our Keira, the light of our eyes. We wanted nothing but the best for her, wanted all her paths to be golden."

Bill shared a look with his wife at her seat near the back of the courtroom. "We may have been the strictest parents a teenage girl ever had, vetting her dates, insisting on curfews, and supervised activities. It was hard on us when she started college and wanted to live on her own, rather than at home with us. But we understood. We didn't like it, but we understood."

He took another swipe at his eyes with his handkerchief. "Then she moved in with a boy. In *my* day, that wasn't done, but young people, well, they do these things. We didn't like it, but she was of age. She didn't ask our permission, just told us what she was doing. Maryanne, well, she shed a tear or two, then told me we'd raised her to make her own decisions, to be independent. Me, I just got mad, but Maryanne wouldn't let me say anything."

Bill turned in his seat to look past the attorney's shoulder to the other table, the one where Mason and his counsel sat. "We met the boy, met him a few times. Never thought much of him. He wasn't good enough for my girl. No sense of responsibility in the boy, no taking charge. But I kept my mouth shut about my opinions. Had to, or my wife would have skinned me alive."

The courtroom crowd chuckled.

He continued. "Then the unforgivable happened."

Staring at her hands, there was no way she could meet

her father's eyes and face the shame and pain she had brought to her parents. "My daughter found herself pregnant, then the two men in her life - her boyfriend and her father, both let her down."

What?

"Her *boy*friend, even though he was an adult, cut and ran out on her as soon as he heard he had created a child with my Keira. Then I, the proud Poppa who at her birth promised to cherish and protect her always, drove her away. I banished her from our home. I was so angry that this had happened to her, how hard her life would now be, that she'd chosen to take up with such a useless specimen of a man that I became a similar man. I let my anger and disappoint take over, saying things I never meant. Harsh things, things I didn't mean."

Now, the handkerchief forgotten, the tears streamed down his cheeks.

Never, not even when her sisters died, had she seen her father cry. Now he was doing it unashamedly in front of an entire group of people. And he looked right at her.

"The next day, my brain returned." He looked toward the back row. "With a few prods from my wife, of course." Chuckles from the rows of people. "But by then it was too late. We looked all over for our Keira, but she was gone, just gone. The college refused to give us any information; she had changed her contact information, so we were not entitled to anything, not any tidbits, even if she still attended there. Her phone number no longer worked. The last address where she lived now housed other people who'd never heard of Keira. She disappeared from our lives, and it was my fault. I banished her. I turned away our only child in her time of need."

Silence, except for the sobs from the man on the stand,

and the echo of similar distress from the back row of the courtroom.

Composing himself, Bill Foster turned to address the room at large. "But you know what my Keira did? She made it. She made it all on her own. She finished college and made a career for herself, for herself and her boy. We are equal parts ashamed of ourselves for making her go it alone and proud of the woman she's become and the fine boy she's raised."

Bill fixed his eyes on the judge. "Your honor, this hearing is about custody and family. Who has been a better custodian of that little boy than my daughter? She did it, she did it all. Put herself through school while pregnant. Had a baby on her own. Built herself a career while caring for a child, and a child with extra needs to boot."

His gaze dwelt on Mason. "Did that young man come back to help her? Not once. Did he call to see how they were doing? Never. Did he grace them with his presence? Did he walk the floors with a colicky baby? Did he put food on their table? Pay the rent? No, not once. Not a single dime did that man ever offer to the mother of his child."

Back to the judge now. "And now, suddenly, eight years after the fact, he wants to be a father. Not only does he want to see his son, be a part of his life, but he wants to take him away from the mother who has been that child's entire world. I ask you, is that fair? Is that justice?"

Chapter Forty-Seven

A knock. A knock *and* the doorbell rang. Someone definitely wanted her attention. Couldn't be Jake; he'd have used his key. Besides, he and Daniel just left for the park fifteen minutes ago.

Through the peephole Keira spied Mason, a fidgety Mason. He raised his finger to push the bell again. Mason. Her least-favorite person in the world. Could she ignore him? Would he go away? He hadn't so far. His knuckles rapped again. Now he yelled, "Keira?"

Oh, just get this over with. She yanked open the door. "What do you want?"

"Daniel…."

"Daniel's not here."

"I'm not here to see Daniel. I came to talk to you."

"I have nothing to say to you. You've done enough damage, you and your lawyer."

"Yeah, about that…" He studied the toe of his sneaker. "Can I come in?"

Oh, what the heck. He'd already done all the harm he could. What was left that he could do to her?

"Look, I've been thinking."

Right. Like that was ever good.

"I might have been wrong."

Ya think?

"Here's the thing. My girlfriend, I mean my wife, Annette, well, she's caught in this will thing. In order for her to inherit, she has to be married with a family, so…"

Ah, now it made sense. Why the sudden wish to claim Daniel.

He studied his hands as he spoke. "That's why we did all this. And her grandmother, well, the old lady's dying, so we had to get a family quick, or Annette wouldn't inherit." He raised his eyes. "You wouldn't believe how many millions we're talking here."

"So, my son was a tool for you to get money."

"Sorta, yeah, I guess you could look at it that way. The old lady said there's no way out - either prove Annette had a family, or the money goes away."

Snort.

"But it's not as bad as it sounds. With all that money, there's a lot to offer Daniel. And he'd eventually inherit everything."

"Until you and Annette had kids of your own, then Daniel'd be shoved out when you longer need him."

Mason shook his head. "No, it's not like that. I'd never do that to him. Besides, Annette can't have kids."

Ka-chink. Now the pieces fell into place.

Mason's eyes met hers directly. "He's my son. And he grows on ya."

True.

"Where is he anyway?"

"He and Jake are at the park. They're meeting my parents there."

"About that. I never knew that you'd fallen out with your parents. I presumed they'd be helping you. You were close."

"Did you think to ask? To check that we were all right?"

Staring at his linked fingers, Mason shook his head. "I was an ass, I admit it. No excuses. I just couldn't handle it, the thought, the responsibility, so I tried not think about it at all. Most of the time it worked."

What do you say to a guy like that?

"Anyway, that's not why I'm here. I got a lawyer, another lawyer, one not connected to Annette's grandmother. Cost me a fortune, but it was worth it."

Oh, no. He'd done it. He'd found a way to take Daniel.

"Apparently, there's no clear definition of family and the concept of family has changed over the years. When that stupid will was made generations ago, it was assumed that family meant a man, woman, and their kids. Nowadays, with half of all marriages ending in divorce, you can have a family, but that doesn't necessarily mean the kids live with you."

What was he getting at?

"See, Daniel doesn't have to live in my house to make him my family. As long as we have some connection, and I'm helping provide for him, he's still my family. Do you get it?"

Not really.

Mason started pacing. "I'm dropping the petition for full custody. I don't need it. I should never have started that. Daniel belongs with you. He loves you, and you're better with him than I am." He stopped directly in front of her. "But he's still my son, too. I want to see him regularly, be a part of his life. I'll pay monthly child support and all the back payments are in an account the lawyers are setting up for you."

"I don't want your money."

"Take it. Use it for whatever. Pay off your house, take a vacation. You deserve it. It's the least I can do."

"Let me make sure I've got this right…"

"The custody petition is off. You are and will always be the custodial parent. But I'm his parent, too. Annette and I are the non-custodial parents. That works for the inheritance requirements and is best for Daniel. All right?"

"So, it's over? It's really over?"

"Yeah, it's over. I'm sorry I put you through this." He wrapped his arms around her for a tight hug. "I'm sorry," he whispered. "You always were too good for me."

Footsteps sounded on the front porch.

Mason wiped his eyes. "Daniel?"

"Probably."

"Is there a back door I can use? I can't let him see me like this."

A key turned in the lock. Daniel and Jake burst through the door, bringing with them the scent of fresh air and sunshine.

Instantly, Jake spotted her wet eyes. "Everything all right?" His cop eyes flicked around the room and down the hallway as Daniel ran to his mom.

"Oh, yes. Is it ever all right!" Surrounded in a group hug by her little man and her soon-to-be husband, every single thing was just fine.

Next in the When Bad Things Happen series

SHARON A. MITCHELL

WHEN BAD THINGS HAPPEN SERIES BOOK 7

SANCTUM

A life beyond redemption. Wait!
That's WRONG. Everyone can be redeemed. Right?

vinci-books.com/SANCTUM

A father's love. A daughter's hope. A soul's last chance at redemption.

Alejandro, desperate to prove his worth and escape his harrowing past, finds himself entangled in a web of his own making. But when his daughter unexpectedly enters his life, Alejandro is forced to confront the demons that have long haunted him. Can the love for his child be the catalyst that breaks the cycle of his past misdeeds?

Turn the page for a free preview…

SANCTUM: Chapter One

1983

"Are you sure?" Jerry's huge frame supported the two little boys swinging from his outstretched arms. He smiled at the older boy, Alex, as the child shrieked in delight. "Me and the missus can keep the kids, and you can send for them once you're settled."

Olivia agreed. "Jerry and I don't mind at all. We'd love to have them."

Janice shook her head. "Thanks, but no. We'll be fine." She hoped.

"Are you sure that you and what's his name don't need a little bit of time to adjust to the new place, just the two of you?"

"No, we'll tackle the surprise together. And his name is Luke."

"Surprise?" Oh, no, thought Olivia. She eyed Janice steadily. "Luke does know that the three of you are coming, doesn't he?"

Janice looked away. "Maybe not exactly, but it'll be okay.

Once he sees the boys, there's not much he can do, is there? I mean, he can't turn us away."

"Oh, Janice, Janice." Jerry ran a hand over his face. "The man doesn't know you have two sons. Really? Are you telling me he expects you to show up alone, that it'll be just the two of you living together?"

Olivia took one of Janice's hands in hers. "Really, the boys will be fine with us if you want to go alone, break the news to this Luke in person, work things out."

"No!" Janice yanked her hand away. "It'll be *fine*, I tell you. It'll all work out. Love me, love my kids, and all that, you know."

Lowering himself to his knees, Jerry let the little boys climb from his arms to his shoulders. With one beefy hand on each child's back, he steadied the two- and four-year-olds, as he walked them to Janice's old beater of a car. Gently, he tucked the kids into the back seat, buckling them into their car seats. To Janice, he said, "Pop the hood, will you?"

As Janice complied, Jerry bent under the hood. "Olivia, bring me two quarts of oil, please, honey?" To Janice, he said, "It's low again. I'll fill it up now and give you an extra quart of oil. But you've got to remember to add oil each time you fill up with gas. Got it?"

"Yeah, I'll remember. I just forgot in all the rush of packing." As Jerry started to speak, she held up her hand. "I know, I know. I get it. You've told me enough times." Looking into the kind face of her neighbor, she altered the tone of her voice. "Jerry, I can't thank you enough. You and Olivia have been so good to us. I'll remember about the oil, I promise. And I'll let you know how we're doing."

With the kids settled in the back seat amid snacks and toys, Janice headed out on I-15 north. It was five hours until they'd get to Las Vegas where she hoped to find a cheap place for them to spend the night, preferably not in the car. She'd planned to get farther than Vegas the first day, but they got a late start. Packing up with two little boys underfoot took more time than she'd anticipated.

But here they were, on their way to a new life. A better life.

She'd miss Olivia and Jerry. They'd been such a help with the boys, always willing to babysit when she had to work shifts at the diner. Well, those times weren't always due to work; sometimes she needed a night out with Luke.

Now, though, they'd be a family, a true family with a mother and a father. Luke would be fine with the boys once he met them. He had to be.

Squawks from the back seat. Matt. For a kid who couldn't talk, he certainly made his feelings known.

"Mom." Alex, ever watchful of his little brother, kicked the back of the driver's seat. "Mom, Matt needs you."

"I can't look now I'm driving. Can't you help him?"

"He stinks. He pooped."

Oh, good grief. The odor reached the front seat now. Could she ignore it?

Less than 10 miles down the road, Alex kicked Janice's seat again. "Mooom. He *really* stinks. And he's mushing it all around."

True, too true. No one could mess a diaper like Mateo. Matt, she corrected herself. While in the US, they used the anglicized forms of their names, rather than their given names. Matt, not Mateo. Janice, not Juana. It's just that being on the road felt like they should be going back home to Rosarito. With a sigh, Janice pulled over to the side of the road.

This had to be her least favorite job in the world. When she'd dreamed of having a baby of her own, *this* had not entered her thoughts.

Pulling her youngest from his car seat, holding him with extended arms, Janice draped Matt on top of her car's trunk. Luckily the temperature was moderate today, so the metal wasn't blisteringly hot. She'd hate to mess up one of their few towels by laying it under him.

Matt squirmed. "No! Hold still." Serve the kid right if he fell off the car. It was his fault they had to stop to deal with this mess.

Geez, the boy was almost three. Would this go on forever?

Matt hated getting his diaper changed. How come? Did he like wallowing in his messes? *She* certainly didn't enjoy this.

Why couldn't he have a normal crap like everyone else? In the toilet, or at least as a solid ball in his diaper. Yeah, that was normal, wasn't it? Not this vile, reeking goo that oozed out every possible crack around his diaper, no matter how tightly she taped the thing onto him.

Janice turned her head away, trying not to gag. She pulled her t-shirt up over her nose, but it gave her little protection against the disgusting stench.

The kid ate the same things as the rest of them. How could he turn it into such a godawful mess? Alex hadn't done this since he was a tiny baby, and certainly not once he was on solid food.

Kicking his legs in the air, Matt grinned up at his mom, those shiny, white front teeth glistening as drool rolled down his cheek. Her heart softened, just a little. He was a cute little devil, took after his father, wherever he was.

That had been a fun few months when she hooked up with that guy in Rosarito, south of the border. She was there introducing 18-month-old Alejandro to his grandmother, Elena. Luckily, the old lady was so thrilled to meet her grandson that she had no problem looking after him while Janice took a much-needed break. Single parenting a toddler was a lot of work, especially when there was no child support or help from the sperm donor, even if he had provided fun while it lasted.

Juana was young; she deserved some fun. It was nice to just be herself again, Juana, rather than assuming the Americanized name, Janice, and pretending to blend in in California. But you did what you had to do.

The result though was this - Matteo. Now she had two boys to look after, all by herself.

Not for long. Soon, Luke would support them. Her mom had always had men to look after her. So far, that had not worked out for Janice, especially after Matteo's birth.

Matt, she reminded herself, not Matteo. Where they were going, fewer people had Hispanic roots. She needed to stick to their American names.

Shoot! Daydreaming didn't pay, especially during a diaper change with Matt. The child wiggled onto his side. With her elbow, Janice rolled him back into position, then lay her forearm across his stomach to hold him in place, while she tugged the soiled diaper from under his bottom.

Shit! Literally. His squirming and the leaky diaper spread filth onto her sleeve as her arm pressed his abdomen to the car. Yanking her arm back, she examined the splotch. Some mocha mush clung to the fabric.

Warning Matt not to move, she squatted down in the

ditch by the side of the road. Plucking handfuls of dried, parched grass, she attempted to remove some of the foul excrement from her shirt. While the chunks scraped off, she succeeded in spreading the puke-brown stain.

A yell from the car made her look up. Alex, turned around in his seat, pointing out the rear window. "Mom, he's gonna fall!"

Bounding up, Janice caught Matt's left arm as he careened off the side of the car. Quickly wrapping her other hand under his armpit, she hoisted the child back onto the trunk of the car. Just about to lay him down, she noticed the telltale brown streak Matt created as he slid off the car.

Grabbing him none too gently, Janice moved to the other side of the car to try again with a fresh spot.

She got the job done. Not well done but done. The kid needed a bath, but there wasn't so much as a puddle around here. If she was home, she'd throw him in the tub and let the water do the job for her. Once when she'd left him playing in the bathtub, she'd returned to find him drinking his bath water, with suspicious brown bits floating all around him. Kids.

For now, she was stuck with diapers and wipes. Wipes were expensive. Didn't the kid realize that? At this rate, they'd run out before they got to Luke's place. The town of Embarrass, Minnesota was a long way away, and she only had so much money to get them through this trip.

SANCTUM: Chapter Two

Janice

Leaving all the windows down for the next half hour helped air out the car's interior. Still the aroma of crap lingered. Old crap. Unhealthy crap, worse than the stench of an unkept, public latrine.

But they were used to it, sort of. It was a fact of life with a kid like Matt. Surely, he'd grow out of this phase soon, and be out of diapers.

It was only one of many things she wished he'd grow out of, albeit this topped the list. As he got older, Alex became easier to look after, more independent, more compliant, seeming to know that he should not make his mother's life any more difficult than it already was. He was a good boy. Matt, on the other hand, didn't seem to get it. There were many things he did not seem to get.

Janice was not the kind of mother to keep baby books, those cutesy pink or blue things where doting parents wrote down notes about when their kid gave a smile unrelated to gas, tried smashed peas, took his first step, said his first word, and stopped needing a diaper. Nope, a single mom, struggling to keep food on the table, didn't have time for such indulgences.

But she didn't remember toilet training Alex being such a big deal. It just sort of happened. Well, maybe Olivia and Jerry had something to do with that, but why didn't they try with Matt as well?

And Janice was absolutely positive that by this age, Alex was talking. He was most certainly walking. Running was more like it.

But three months shy of his third birthday, Matt did none of these things.

The desert landscape had never been her thing. Although her hometown of Rosarito was arid, there was the nearby ocean. San Diego was more than just shades of brown as well.

Dotting the highway, small towns appeared, then disappeared in her rearview mirror. They got in the way when the highway wound right through them, causing traffic to slow to a crawl.

Don't complain. She could hear Olivia's voice in her ear. See this as an opportunity. She was moving to a small town to be with Luke, so maybe she should learn to appreciate the treasures towns offered.

Like that. An ancient Victorian, three-storey house stood out, a painted lady amid drab browns. Exotic with vibrant purple shutters alongside each window, wraparound porches with swings and rocking chairs. Sanctum. What a name for a bed and breakfast. A sanctuary. If she was by herself, she'd be tempted to stop at such a place. But no, she needed to keep going, get to Luke and the life they had planned together. There she'd find her own sanctum, a place of her own. Smiling, she sped up and continued her journey.

Pulling over, Janice scrolled through the travel guidebook Olivia gave her, searching for a Vegas hotel room that would fit her budget. The first ten minutes were discouraging. She shouldn't have to choose between giving them a place to sleep and eating, should she?

"Quit it!" She hollered at Alex, whose little feet thumped away at the back of her seat. "I'm trying to find us a hotel room."

"But Mom, Matt and me are hungry."

"Aren't we all?"

The kid didn't let up, almost drowning out Matt's howls. Kids. Opening her door, Janice left the car. Nope, she still couldn't hear herself think about the racket her sons made. Back in the driver's seat, she pressed the buttons to raise all the windows, then turned off the ignition.

There. Now it was quieter out here. The boys weren't silent by any means, but muffled, so she could concentrate. It would get hot in the car, yeah, but if she could just concentrate, she'd have this figured out quickly and turn the air conditioning back on as they got on their way.

What? Had she missed something? Quickly she flipped back, and yes, there it was. Something in the 30s. Yes! That was the price range she could handle. But wait. Were there resort fees? Those things could double the price for the room.

She read aloud:

RIO Las Vegas Hotel Suites

Our over 500 sq. ft. Luxury Masquerade Suites feature two queen beds with floor-to-ceiling windows offering spectacular sunset views of Las Vegas's Spring Mountains. Amenities include mini-refrigerator, sofa, flat screen TV with On Demand movies, in-room safe, iron/board and hair dryer.

Rates From ~~$36~~ $32

And would you look at that picture? Wow! Even if the photo was taken a decade ago, it was still nicer than anything she'd ever stayed in before. And the size - it was almost as big as her whole apartment had been. Two beds, so she wouldn't have to put up with getting kicked by restless, sleeping little boys all night. The hair dryer meant that she could wash the shirt she wore and make sure it was dried enough to wear tomorrow. She raised her arm toward her face and took a sniff. Yep. It was not just the nasty brown stain that offended her. Maybe she could wash the back of Matt's shirt as well where some of the noxious excrement had seeped onto it.

No resort fees. Free parking. Restaurants on site. That meant she didn't have to drag two kids through the teeming streets of Vegas to feed them. Matt was so heavy to carry far. When would that kid learn to walk?

Janice pulled off at the next exit, found a phone booth, and rang the hotel. It would be just her luck to have this amazing room all sold out before she could get there. But no, she was in luck for once in her miserable life. Maybe things were truly turning around. She was on her way to a new life with a great guy who would look after her, plus she had an amazing room in which to spend the night. It was an omen of better things to come.

Luke

It was cold. Colder than anything he'd experienced in his life. Colder than any human could be expected to survive. Did people actually *choose* to live in places like this? And they told him winter had barely begun here in Embarrass, Minnesota, one of the coldest places in the continental USA.

The sensations created by the arctic air started with just a tingling at the ends of his fingers, then sank deeper into his sinews and tendons until they ignited in a bizarre combination of blazing fire and numbing ice at the same time.

Removing his right glove, Luke blew on his hand, flexing his fingers to get some life back into his frozen digits. Maybe not frozen. The guys told him that when something froze you couldn't feel it any longer. Nope, the pain in his fingers meant his hand was not frozen, just damned cold.

Cursing, he put the glove back on, tightening the Velcro closure at the wrist. He'd learned not to let cold air leak between his sleeve and the decent work gloves provided by the company. Thank God for this one perk. His own gloves had holes in them, and he had to double the fabric over when he clung to the steering wheel of the old beater of a truck his grandmother left him.

Things got tough in San Diego. It wasn't so bad until he lost his job. Not his fault that the company folded. Times were hard and lots of businesses struggled. That didn't mean *he* had to, did it? Yeah, apparently it did. There were no jobs to be found and his meagre savings dwindled faster than the under-counter kegs at his fave drinking hole.

Then came the news that he'd inherited his grandmother's house. He hardly knew her, just some vague memories of playing at her place as a boy.

Those were good times. Back then his dad and mom got along. Visiting Gran was great - a road trip, staying at hotels, eating in restaurants, then running free through the fields surrounding her tiny farmhouse.

Life changed, though, as it's wont to do. Sucks, but what can you do? Dad lost his job in the oil patch, and things got harder around home, leaner. The old man never found a job to adequately replace that salary. Mom's work at the cleaners kept food on the table, mostly. Food and booze, in varying proportions, depending on the mood in the household at any given time.

Luke was not a big man and that was on his parents' shoulders. They'd rather drink than fill their son's belly with the food he needed to reach his potential.

Now he was taxed to keep up with his workmates. The heavy branches some hauled with ease required supreme effort from Luke. He hated that he grunted under their weight, but sometimes he couldn't control it. That's the extent of the bellyaching he allowed himself.

At first, working for a tree trimming company seemed great. Breezes from the lake moderated the August temperatures. For a guy who hated being cooped up, this was the ideal job. Decent people to work with, an okay wage, and a boss who promised to give him as many hours as he could.

Pity that he had to work at all, but such was life. He'd hoped that inheriting a house had meant a little money with it as well.

Nope. Yeah, he got the land and house all right, such as it was.

The place in his memories twenty some years past was small, but quaint. Space to run, to ride the rickety bike stored in an old shed that listed to one side. That shed was cool; when he pushed on its side with all his might, he could make the building creak and sway. His mom ordered him to never go in there, but the place was full of treasures, including the bike.

Well, now that building was a heap of twisted and splintered timbers on the ground. Not even rats found it habitable these days. Maybe there were a few treasures buried in the rubble, maybe one day he'd poke around.

For now, he needed to make a living. Sure, there was no rent to pay, but he still had to eat. And, as winter approached, the house leaked frigid air. Yesterday when he woke up, the glass of water beside his bed had a skiff of ice on top. Heating the place was going to be a bummer for sure this winter.

While his boss was flush with tree trimming contracts in the summer and fall, they'd slowed to a trickle now. The only times Luke got called to come work recently was when tree branches went down in a storm. Like now. Perched in the truck's damned utility bucket, high above the ground, arms extended to run a chainsaw that weighed more than the boulders lining the walk to his front door, freezing off parts of his anatomy he'd rather keep.

Don't think about it. Just get the job done and get down from this perch.

He'd never met his grandfather. Word had it, he used to farm the land around the house. Some grain, some hay, some animals. Something to think about, maybe a way to make some good cash. How hard could it be?

Soon Janice would be here. She'd find work easily; women could always do stuff in towns like this. Stores, two diners, cleaning houses, there was plenty of work for her. Her income would see them through the lean times when he didn't get many shifts.

SANCTUM: Chapter Three

Unbelievable! The most beautiful place she'd ever seen. Who'd have thought that one day she'd stay in digs like this? Yes, things were looking up.

Twirling slowly in place, Janice took it all in. Floor-to-ceiling windows filled one wall. In the distance were Las Vegas' Spring Mountains. Below, the city spread out in all its glory. Soon night would fall, bringing a panorama of twinkling lights. She filled her lungs. Even the air in the room smelled fresh. No mold. No rust. No rotting food in a trash can.

Peeking into the bathroom, she saw nothing but sparkling white fixtures and fluffy, folded towels. Not one of them on the floor, not a thing out of place.

Back in the main room, Alex squealed in delight, jumping on the queen-sized bed. Matt managed to climb up but lacked the balance to mimic his brother. Instead, he sat as close as he could to Alex's jumping feet, shrieking with glee as each bounce knocked him over.

To the side of the room were two easy chairs, plusher

than any she'd ever hoped to own. The deep, dark brown carpet surrounded and comforted her tired feet. Near the seating area a large TV commanded attention.

Not bad, not bad at all. Maybe they should stay here two nights.

Sinking into one of the comfy chairs, she switched on the TV, put her feet on the matching ottoman, and ignored her sons.

It worked for a while, but not nearly long enough.

Matt started his mewling noises. He didn't have a wide range of verbal communication strategies. This particular noise could mean two things - either he needed something put into his mouth, or he'd evacuated something from the other end. In, out, in, out. It never ended.

Her nose gave the air a sniff. Nope, nothing wafted this way yet.

"Mom, we're hungry."

Ah, Alex interpreted his brother's complaint and echoed it.

"In a bit." She put her head back down against the chair back and pointed the remote at the giant TV. She'd give herself another five minutes of relaxation. That wasn't too much to ask, was it?

Apparently.

The bouncing stopped and the boys left the bed to drape themselves over their mother.

Peace was over. From experience, when her sons got *hangry*, things went from bad to worse.

Pulling open the desk drawer, she inspected the options at the Rio. No sense going somewhere in the car then needing to find a parking spot again. And she certainly wasn't walking the Strip with her kids when she had to carry Matt.

The cheapest option looked like Smashburger. Something a kid would eat and how bad could their prices be for a burger?

At least service was prompt and there weren't many people in the restaurant. But, that much for a burger? For a kid? By the time she bought them hamburgers, fries, and sodas, their steal-of-a-deal hotel room didn't look quite such a bargain. She picked fries from the boys' plates, knowing they'd be unable to finish some of their meals, especially Matt. She'd eat whatever they left. In the meantime, she splurged on a beer for herself, something local they had on tap. It was okay, but she'd have preferred a Bud.

Back in the room, she stuck the boys in the bathtub, marveling at how clean it was. How did you even get porcelain that shiny?

Knowing they'd amuse themselves for a good half hour, she tucked her feet under her and settled into the soft chair cushions to flick through the channels on the TV. Hmm. Disappointingly similar to the channels she got at home.

Still, it was lovely just being here. The hotel had generously stocked the minibar for her. She emptied the contents, lining up tiny bottles of vodka, rum, and bourbon for later, and the chocolate bars and bags of chips as bedtime treats for the boys. On second thought, she hid the bars and chips in a drawer. They'd do for breakfast, saving her money tomorrow.

The boys' sounds were muted through the closed bathroom door. Inky blackness enveloped the floor-to-ceiling windows, with lights twinkling in the darkness, illuminating the never still Strip. Tempting to stay here in this room, pretend this was her life, even for just a few days.

She sipped on her beer from the mini bar and considered. No, with food this expensive, they couldn't afford to spend a second night in Vegas. Pity.

Grab your copy...
vinci-books.com/SANCTUM

About the Author

Sharon A. Mitchell lives on a farm, with her nearest neighbor several miles away. Does that seem like a setting to spark the imagination? It does for her.

When she's not writing her numerous thriller series, she can be found taking long walks with her hundred-pound German Shepherd dogs, Pickles and Dill. (She didn't name them - don't blame her.)